The Road Les.

Short Stories
by

Boris Finkelstein

For My Grandchildren

From author and grandfather of your student Olha Babushkina-Fynkelshtern as a present to Rye St. Antony school.

11.11.2022

About the Author

Boris Finkelstein is an author, engineer, banker and extreme sports fanatic. He has written fifteen books of Russian language short stories, which have been translated into into Ukrainian, Crimean Tatar, French, and now English. He is a member of the National Writers' Union of Ukraine, and the Union of Journalists of Ukraine. He headed the Crimean branch of the National Writers' Union of Ukraine until Russia illegally annexed the peninsula in 2014. He has received numerous literary awards, including the State Prize of Crimea.

Boris was born in 1946, in Odesa on Ukraine's Black Sea coast and was a maths prodigy. He worked as a banker in Crimea during the wild years of the nineties when banks were targeted by machine-gun wielding Mafiosi. He has worked as an engineer, served as a soldier, and lived in several Ukrainian and Russian cities. His long and varied career and wide ranging interests give him a wealth of exciting material for his short stories. "The Road Less Travelled By" is the first English language translation of his work.

Contents

Probability and Me

The probability of an event in a given experiment, according to the classical definition, is the ratio of the number of experimental outcomes conducive to the event, in relation to the total number of outcomes that compose a whole group of equally probable, but mutually exclusive, events. You cannot discard words from songs, as the saying goes, but sometimes weird things happen in life.

In 1958, when I was twelve, a breath of fresh air, which would later be known as the 'Khrushchev thaw', wafted over the country. Strangely enough, this also affected the sphere of mathematics and the country suddenly needed specialists in the field of science, previously known as 'the whore of capitalism'. These areas included cybernetics, genetics and probability theory, among others whose names sounded odd to the limited mentality of the time. As usual, new times came and the people had to be answerable to someone who in a previous era would have been nervously catching their breath.

My father was the head of the mathematics department at the Astrakhan Pedagogical Institute. He had been placidly specialising in theoretical mechanics, differential and integral calculus, and other apolitical disciplines, but under the thaw he had been instructed to prepare and read a course in probability theory. This kind of free thinking was unheard of at the time so he was a little confused and concerned about this change and unguardedly told his family about it over dinner.

It would not be difficult for him to move from his existing working practises, he had been a child prodigy born with mathematical gifts, but it was a painful surprise to him. What had previously been frowned upon was now going to form part of his lectures. He wondered who would be blamed if everything returned to how it had been, but had no choice other than to carry out the instructions because most of the other certified and ideologically sound colleagues at the mathematics department did not have the same level of skill. Their abilities would not have allowed them to rise above a simple Soviet-Communist Party course or that of a ministerially approved high school textbook. His reflection apparently took some time but, like a sound and sensible individual, my father scheduled it into his future plans and set to work.

"Look Grigorii Markovich, this theory has existed for quite a while in a hostile ideological environment and it requires a very lucid reference to the theory and practice of socialist construction," they told him at the party committee.

My father thought about what a marvellous beginning this was for his project and remembered the ideological disputes that had previously seethed around the materialistic foundations of socialist theory. More precisely, he remembered the lack of such squabbles in the area of probability and random processes. He decided that his first task should be to verify empirically what was probable in the material world. The experimental base was very limited. He emerged from his study and, looking around, found me hunkered down with a book by the window.

"Son, we have to prove or disprove a mathematical theory."

I understood nothing of what he said, but decided it was best to keep quiet. After his baffling statement my father gave me five kopecks and said, "Go into the yard and flip this coin one hundred times. If probability exists, then the coin will land with heads or tails upwards roughly the same number of times."

"And if it doesn't exist?" I asked timidly.

"Well, then throw it another one hundred times and probability must eventually manifest itself," he replied.

I did not want to toss a coin but, hoping to sort this out for him quickly, I embarked upon the process. The ratio was roughly forty-eight to fifty-two. He approved the result but said that we should give it another one hundred tosses just to confirm this. At this point I kicked up a fuss. I thought about all the things I needed to do to get out of doing the experiment: the uncompleted homework, the friend I needed to see to work on our Russian etc.

My father knew that the experiment must capture my imagination. He had grown up on the streets of Odesa, in the Moldavanka district, and recollected the innocent gambling of his childhood. "Let's play a game," he said, "if it lands on tails more, I win and you will toss it another one hundred times. If it lands on heads more, I lose and I'll give you one rouble."

His proposal was very interesting to me because one rouble was serious money back then. I thought about my potential new wealth and began to throw the coin, but lost by a huge ratio of sixty to forty.

"It hasn't worked out for you," my father said in surprise. "What's happened to probability? Toss it some more."

But the next time the result was even worse. "You know what," he said, "I'll give you one rouble anyway, as payment for your work, and we'll agree that if tails comes out on top we'll stop."

I was really becoming bored with this now, but to appease my father and make myself some money I tossed the coin another one hundred times and reverse probability immediately proved its existence. At this point my father discovered a law. "Yes," he said, "probability manifests as a pattern in a random process; however, you somehow managed to reduce the probability of an event you desired."

It is worth noting at this point that I've always had bad luck when gambling, so bad that it is not worth me playing. However, this did enable my father to reach a conclusion that has stuck with me to this day. "Don't trust your luck son - Ever. Prepare your activities, ensure the results are guaranteed and place your plans beyond the limits of probability estimates.

Then you'll be fine."

He was right; I have carried on like that for fifty years and it has really helped. Give it a try.

Parade–allee…

It was the winter of 1957 and the weather in Astrakhan was freezing. I was ten years old and staring through the classroom window; I was thoroughly bored during the second lesson devoted to our 'native language', and was lost in thought. The periphery of the window was rimmed with thin strips of white paper to keep in the heat, but it was letting us down badly. My desk was on the back row and the place next to me was empty. At first I wanted to sleep, but then I started to mentally prepare for a fight in the break. I regularly fought with the other boys, maybe two or three times a week; it was conflict planning, you could say, for a 'place in the sun'.

The truth was I had a serious opponent that day; he was much bigger than me and an experienced rascal whose poor academic performance had resulted in him repeating the course. This meant he was at least one year older than me, and it showed. However, the idea of surrender never even entered my head.

"Finkelstein," the voice of the teacher echoed from far away at the front of the class, "please continue."

"Excuse me, Aleksandra Ivanovna," I said, standing up, "where shall I start reading from?"

"Start here," she said, and uttered the last two words of a piece we had been given as homework. I had spent the whole of the previous evening playing hockey and skating so had only skimmed the three pages we had been given as homework at the start of the lesson. Fortunately, I had an amazing memory back then, I closed my eyes and the relevant page of the textbook appeared in front of me. All I had to do was read it out.

"Sit," said the teacher, disappointed by my success. "Yet more good behaviour that you haven't paid for," she added.

I kept quiet. There were big problems with my behaviour, which was why I was sitting on my own. I had been involved in a fight with the last child I had sat next to, so was moved to the back of the class.

We were interrupted by the sound of footsteps echoing in the corridor before the classroom door swung open and the one-armed headmaster, a disabled veteran, shunted himself sideways into the room. A skinny, blond boy of my age followed behind him. "Take this pupil into your class, Aleksandra Ivanovna," he ordered in the commanding baritone befitting a headmaster, before spinning around and disappearing through the door. The boy remained standing, clutching his briefcase with both hands and staring at his new classmates with wide eyes.

"What's your name?" the teacher asked him.

"Sergei," said the new boy timidly, "Sergei Pavlov."

"Well, find yourself a seat."

There were only two unoccupied places in the class. One was next to me, the other was next to a very plump girl called Tamara. Sergei had no knowledge of my bad reputation and it was not considered cool to sit next to a girl when in the fourth grade, so he crossed the room and sat next to me.

During the break I had my fight with the loser who had been forced to repeat the course. The result of our scuffle was unclear and the audience's opinion was divided.

After I had let off some steam I chatted to my new neighbour and found that everything about him was much more interesting than I had previously thought. Sergei was from a circus family and the troupe his mother and father performed in was known as the Ivanov Aerial Acrobats.

"Why Ivanov," I asked, "when your surname is Pavlov?"

"It's a pseudonym, a circus name," said Sergei, embarrassed, "so we have adopted it."

"What was your grandfather's real name?"

"Bull, Henryk Bull," he said timidly, "but after the revolution it was hard to live with that surname."

14

I understood that perfectly well, it was not easy for my family with our surname either.

One way or another we quickly became staunch friends. I stopped going to hockey practise and started going to the circus with him after school. It was not the kind of circus I was used to seeing; there were no spectators, no orchestra and no gaudy festivities; it was a peek behind the scenes, but a fascinating peek.

The circus tent was a huge, canvas big top and nearby there were wagons, with all the equipment required by a circus, and the animals. There were three parts to the troupe's programme; stunt horse riding, the world championship in Greco-Roman wrestling, and the renowned aerial acrobats themselves. Every evening the Ivanov Aerial Acrobats performed in the arena; there were only three of them, Sergei and his mum and dad. A further three performers in the troupe were young graduates of the circus academy. Sergei only performed on Sundays before an audience of children, due to his age, but he was a still an artist.

I attended rehearsals every day with Sergei and very quickly became a part of the life of the circus. It was not long before I was being asked to fetch oats for the horses or get some beer; I soon became one of their own.

I was particularly interested in the wrestlers, who were sturdy, hefty men aged between forty to fifty years old. I realised that in the past they had been in some real wrestling matches. They did not rehearse their fights, instead they practised some strange semi-acrobatic tricks, which seemed bizarre to me. It soon became clear when I stayed behind one evening and watched their display from behind the curtains that it was a real spectacle. Of course, I did not know the word then, but it had nothing to do with the sport of wrestling.

Two wrestlers came out at the start; one large and hefty, the other smaller and of meagre stature. The heavier man threw the skinnier one around for a long time, but could not flip him on to his shoulders. At the right moment the fat man became caught on the mat and fell, the small one jumped deftly and, the horror of it, fatty's shoulders hit the mat. Touché! The circus burst into applause, music thundered from somewhere, and everyone cheered. Another fighter, a big, black-moustached man, entered the ring and dispatched all his opponents quickly and mercilessly. The victor then invited participants from the audience to have a try at claiming the prize from him. An idiot in a typical soviet-era padded jacket stepped forward and stripped down to his large pair of underpants. Amazingly, he defeated the victor.

Fanfares blared before the unconquered fighter known as 'Black Mask' (not a very original name when one considered the facial covering he always wore) entered the arena ceremoniously. Black Mask always vanquished everyone. However, for the past fortnight fly posters plastered all over the city announced that he was throwing down a challenge to the wrestler known as Red Mask.

The palaver of the circus usually went on for three or four months then it left and pitched up in a new location. This unstable existence meant that my friend Sergei often changed schools and could never spend time on the core curriculum. Even though I was a trouble maker I thought that Sergei missing out on his education was unfair. I lived continuously in the same place, had a separate room to study in and had unpaid consultants in the form of my parents, who were mathematicians. I made it my goal to help my new friend and began to invite him home and explain the lessons to him. After a while he began to get a four grade, which was the end point of the fourth class in high school. Although I messed around at school and almost never studied, I read a lot; possibly even too much.

I enjoyed being with my new friend, one month passed,

then another, and suddenly, on a day early in March, Sergei failed to turn up at school. "Boris, go and find out what's wrong," the teacher instructed.

After lessons were over I went to visit the circus to find out what had happened to Sergei. When I arrived I found he was ill with a high temperature and a sore throat. His parents were very concerned for him, but they were even more worried about the possibility of having to cancel the children's show on Sunday. There were only two parts to the junior's show and one of them was aerial acrobatics which featured performances by Sergei. Watching someone their age excited the children and the success of the whole show rested on him.

When Saturday arrived it was clear that there was no way Sergei would be well enough to perform the next day. There were no other boys in the troupe, so his parents had been discussing what would happen for quite a while. Sergei's father looked at me and interest flickered in his eyes, "Perhaps you could take part in the display?"

Despite my not in the least childlike arrogance, I was totally non-plussed. "Me, an acrobat? Ha-ha!"

"Well, no," Sergei's father continued, "you'll just stand on the platform and we'll do the rest." I remembered that two tiny platforms with a rope strung between them were usually eight metres above the arena. "Don't worry," he said, "we'll stick you on the second platform, you won't be moving anywhere and you'll bail out your friend. We can't lose our spectators." Sergei's father winked at me conspiratorially and said, "You're both of the same height, no one will tell you apart from a distance."

"Why not, he's blond?" I muttered in surprise.

"That's nothing, we'll powder your bonce. And anyway, who comes to the show twice to compare you two?"

Those words sealed it and I made an immediate decision. "OK," I said, "but only this once."

"Just once, only once," said Sergei's parents, nodding

delightedly. "He'll have recovered by next Sunday."

We spent the next two hours rehearsing. Nothing was as simple as it had appeared, even standing on a platform and, strangely, even bowing to the audience seemed hard, but I did not need to do that.

The following day I told my family that I was going to play hockey and, with my ice skates laced together and slung over my shoulder, I headed for the circus where they dressed me in a sequinned costume, powdered my hair, took me by the hand and I found myself behind the curtain.

"The show begins! Parade-allee!" a voice thundered.

The circus march blared out, the curtain parted and I realised the show was beginning. There was no turning back now, the brilliantly illuminated circus lay before us with thousands of pairs of eyes staring at me. I froze, but everything was already swirling around me. I felt myself being pulled along by my hand before I was released, but my legs would not obey me; although I was moving along somehow. To the right and left of me, gymnasts from the Ivanov troop bowed and rose. They ardently stretched out their arms to their worthy spectators and then suddenly spun around and ran back behind the scene. If someone had not grabbed me by the hand and dragged me off, I would probably have remained standing in the arena.

When I finally realised what had happened I laboriously opened my mouth and asked, "Is that it then?"

"No, let's go, we're on," said someone.

Everything became like an incredible dream. I stepped out, ascended the stairs, someone clipped a safety harness with a rope to me, and our performance started. After a few minutes I was able to relax and release the bar I had been gripping frantically. I was even calm enough to observe with interest how Sergei's father and another acrobat threw Sergei's mother between them. Such behaviour from parents was a novelty for me. Both my parents were academics; my father taught at the

Institute of Mathematics and my mother was a school teacher. I had no idea anyone's parents could carry on like that.

I looked into the arena and realised I had never seen so many people before. Okay, I had been at demonstrations but there the people had not been looking at me, and how they stared at me now. Suddenly, I saw, among this sea of faces, as through a pair of binoculars, two familiar eyes, it was a small boy from our residential block who was there with his father. He spotted me and jumped up and yelled with delight, stretching his hands towards me. A bad feeling welled up inside me and I knew my parents were sure to fine out about my antics.

The performance ended, I was dressed in my usual clothes and I stood passively as they took off my make up and thanked me. As I was leaving to return home I heard one of them say, "That boy's got pluck; his first time before an audience and he coped."

A commission was waiting for me when I arrived home; to say there was a scandal would be totally inadequate. My mother could have managed a scandal on her own, but what surprised me was that my usually taciturn father was in a state of shock. "My son, my son, lowering himself to appear in the circus," he kept repeating in a tragic whisper. My mother, who had previously said I would end up as a cobbler if I did not study, had totally revised her dismal prediction. Now I was going to end up as a clown.

My attempts to justify myself failed and I was deprived of all kinds of desirable things for the foreseeable future and dispatched to my room to sleep. Thankfully, I had a torch so I was still able to read by putting my head under the blanket. In the quietness of my room I could eavesdrop on my parents as they berated each other and made plans to improve the rigour of my future education.

The fact that my parents were not thrilled with me did not bother me in the least. My father was working double time at the institute and did not return home until nine or ten in the evenings, so I escaped his wrath. My mother was busy with my younger brother, who was just over one month old, so I was pretty much left to myself. I did not pay much heed to the housekeeper, who showed up occasionally, because I was quite an independent boy and able to stand up for myself. Six years after this event I left home for good and only returned and departed as a guest.

The circus and Sergei left town three weeks later and we never saw each other again, but something remained with me. The same courage and will-power that actors have when performing dangerous stunts. I needed these qualities for several years when I was in difficult and risky situations and find I sometimes still need them. Long after the events in this tale I read Edmond Rostand's play, Cyrano de Bergerac and was particularly struck by the lines:

Let me introduce them to you!
They are dear to me as memory.
Falsehood! Villainy! Envy! Hypocrisy!
And who else? I am not a coward.
I will at least not surrender
And I will die fighting.

These lines became one of my mottos for a long time and, possibly, forever - All because of my brief childhood career as a circus acrobat.

The Corporal's Stick

At the age of six, I moved with my parents from Odesa to the larger city of Astrakhan. It was a different, very depressing, world for me; there was no sea and I loved the sea. The climate in the lower Volga region was terrible; it was cold and windy with hardly any snow in winter, and very hot in summer. It was only bearable during spring and autumn. On top of this, the relationships between people, both adults and children, were very different in this city. I was accustomed to the noisy, but in actuality, gentle and ironic dialogue in Odesa and could not understand the unconcealed hostility that greeted me in my new habitat.

When I was older I understood there were different traditions there. Not everyone under forty in the areas that were once occupied under the Soviet Union understands this. Our lives were dominated by horrible inhuman slogans such as, *'Whoever is not with us is against us'* or *'If the enemy doesn't surrender, destroy them'*. The slogans contained veiled threats; one, which encouraged children to inform on their parents, ran, *'The son is not responsible for his father'*, and there were many others which dominated and controlled our lives, such as, *'If the party says it's necessary, the Komsomol will take responsibility'*. The Komsomol were the young communists who were building socialism; the young pioneers were the soviet answer to the scout movement. Instead of the motto 'be prepared' they had the motto, 'always prepared', but prepared for what?

The practical implications of all this were very simple; whoever did not agree or did not adhere completely to the principles would be weeded out. A vast number of people were incarcerated in camps or forced to work on building sites in a kind of labour army, often in a frozen wasteland. Working for the state was compulsory and people were distributed centrally and transferred from one place to another. Any other way of life

21

was considered parasitism or desertion; it was as if we were an army and would have very serious consequences.

Once upon a time, in a place not so far away, people understood that survival was not very easy. Life was extremely harsh and was ruled by severe laws, both written and unwritten. Those who survived and were liberated carried these rules over into ordinary life. Astrakhan was a place whose denizens would not usually be allowed into the European part of the country. Then it was said, *'Life here is like in a henhouse, peck the one next to you and spit on them below'*, or perhaps, *'Life is like an acorn in the forest – there are wolves and oaks all around, and every pig can eat'*. This oral folklore reflected our life; all these dismal sayings were actually put into practice and that is what was really unpleasant about it.

My parents were allocated two rooms in a three-storey hall of residence at the teaching college. Students and the families of lecturers lived there. There was another three-storey building further along the street, but this was an entirely different kinds of residential blocks. Our block was inhabited by relatively well-off adults and their children; the other block was occupied by people who were considerable less well-off. The disadvantaged children were much more organised than we, the offspring of decent folk, were and had been running as pack where the laws of the wolf ruled for a long time. When I ventured out on to the street I often found myself face to face with one of these aggressive neighbours and these encounters usually ended badly. Apart from going to school, I practically never ventured outside the courtyard of our block.

When I went to school my route ran right past that very same, ominous, building. My parents could not understand why I always came home with scratches and bruises on my face, a torn handle on my briefcase, spilled ink, without my cap, and with my buttons torn off. They ascribed all this to my pugnacious and quarrelsome nature. However, one day, when I had finished the third class, my mother, who worked as a teacher at the school, was returning home at the same time. She found a bunch of small children gathered by our fence; I rolled out from them to her feet, battered but unbeaten. They all scarpered and I remained on the ground, wearing only one sandal; the buckle had broken on the other one and it had flown off in the heat of the battle. The truth of my predicament was out and my parents gathered a family council. Accompanying me to and from school was not an option because no one had the time, and I would never have let myself be shamed like that.

My father had grown up on the streets of Odesa without a father and understood what was going on. "Where are your friends?" he asked. "There are a lot of you living in our apartment block, why don't you go around together and help each other?"

The more I thought about it, the more it seemed like an interesting and practical idea. However, I doubted the martial capabilities of the neighbouring children in our block. But why not give them a try? In the evening I gathered as many of them as I could in the yard and gave them a rousing speech, "Lads, there are a lot of us too; are we worse than them? Let's talk to them in the same language they use. Let's change things around here, let's give 'em the thrashing they deserve."

A couple left quickly and it was clear they did not want to be involved in my gang, but my words roused some of the others. The next day six of us returned home together from school. We were so close, just one hundred metres and we would have been in our own yard, but none of us made it. A few youngsters emerged from the entrance to the rival block and, smiling unpleasantly, headed for us. "Forward," I yelled and, throwing my briefcase aside, rushed into the fray. The skirmish was, as usual, brief and somewhere far ahead of us flashed the heels of my scarpering comrades.

"Yeah," the leader of our foes said sympathetically as he

shunted me in the ribs yet again, "your boys aren't fighters."

I picked up my briefcase and went home. As I licked my wounds, ever more fantastic plans for revenge ripened in my mind. However, having calmed down, I decided to deal with the matter scientifically and study the relevant theories. I spent many hours rooting around my father's library, but found nothing useful; just some mathematics journals and other publications to which he subscribed.

I decided to widen my field of research and headed to the city library. To the amazement of the old ladies working there, I did not choose the fairy tales popular with those my age, instead I took books from the military science section. I found nothing useful at first but after a while I began to form a curious opinion about the material I read. It seemed to me that it was worth studying the Russian and soviet authors. According to the historical tomes on the shelves, they always thrashed the Germans and Swedes. But something about this confused me. Finally, I understood. The victories had been in wars fought not only by armed units and armies but also by the whole people, who were, as a rule, poorly trained and armed; but these vast losses were somehow overlooked. The Russian chiefs, Minin and Pozharsky, the Napoleonic and both world wars, and even, as I understood from one textbook, the triumph over tiny Finland had required a mass mobilisation. Was a triumph at the price of so many lives really a victory? And our foes? The foes usually only deployed an army consisting of paid, professional soldiers. So, we could not triumph with a small force, we could only die heroically, and I had already been through that.

Even though I was only ten years old, my awareness of how Russia waged war made me determined to read about its foes. I found a respectable book entitled *The History of Fredrick the Great* and read it from cover to cover. I remember how deeply I was impressed by 'Old Fritz's' saying that the soldier must be more scared of the corporal's stick than the foe. I knew what I had to do. I had to become a corporal.

I summoned my close comrade, Tolia, into the yard; he who had fled the enemy before anyone else. "Tolia," I asked, "why did you run?"

"I was scared," he replied innocently.

He was not alone in his simple honesty. Khrushchev had replied similarly when a zealous journalist asked him about Stalinism, with the words, "So you knew about all this earlier and did nothing?" From that moment forth even grown men could acknowledge cowardice without blushing in shame. And here we were talking about children.

"Great, Tolia," I said, "now you're going to be more scared of me than the enemy." I threw myself at him and gave the poor boy a severe beating. "Get this Tolia," I admonished him, having executed my sentence on his cowardice, "if you scarper again I'll thrash you on a daily basis."

This procedure was repeated with all six of the participants in the debacle. I was so carried away by the end that I even hammered four other boys who had not participated in the previous fight, one at a time.

One week later, I led my army of ten variously aged thugs into the last and most decisive skirmish. We accepted the challenge of the battle and we lost. No, no one ran away. We just discovered that decent children have no idea how to fight. Bruised, scratched and roaring with dismay and shame we beat a retreat.

I once again began reflecting seriously on military matters as I approached the sawmill in the rather large yard of our residential block. The carpenter who worked there was called Vasia; he was a sturdy chap with a wooden leg, having lost his original leg in the war when, as he told me, he worked as a regimental intelligence officer. The mere lack of a leg did not prevent him from bustling around, regularly getting inebriated and being the sweetheart of all the ladies nearby. Men who had fought had a hard time after the war, but he was an honest fellow and I shared what had happened with him. He quickly cut to the chase, "So, they thrash you all the time? They're fascists!" He was outraged and said, "Bring the boys here, I'll give them a little training."

Vasia had not been lying; on the basis of what happened it soon became clear that he really had been a regimental intelligence officer. I remember a couple of his, far from childish, tricks to this day.

"The main thing," said Vasia, "is to move swifter than the foe. He who is faster wins. And he who wins is right."

One week later we went into battle for the third time. The foe was defeated and fled; victory was ours. This triumph was hugely inspirational for my squad. We began to penetrate deeper into enemy territory. We recruited a couple of companies from the neighbouring private housing and finally became a serious threat to public order. A district official visited my parent and 'had a word' with them. It transpired they had received complaints from more than one of the parents of the disadvantaged children. My father summoned me for an educational conversation. "Why did it enter your head to organise a group of hooligans? And with children from good families! Who put you up to it?"

"You," I replied innocently, "you gave me the idea. Thank you."

Life continued, my parents moved me to another school. There was a different group of children there and life settled down. But something inside me had changed forever.

"Vasia," I said to the carpenter when we were sitting together at the sawmill, "do you know why our children didn't scarper the second time?" He shook his head and I imparted my new found knowledge about the principles of Frederick, the Great, the greatest commander of the Seven Year War.

"Marvellous," said Vasia, "we have known this for a long

time. Thrash your own folk so others are afraid of you." And he jumped on the wooden plank in front of the circular saw.

I remembered this logical conclusion very well. Later, when I was studying at the institute, I posed this question to an elderly colonel from the military faculty during a seminar. "Are there any military personnel in your family?" he asked, suddenly becoming very serious.

"No, mathematics is much more their thing," I replied.

I was intrigued when he gave me a book by an English military historian the following day. It was entitled *The Strategy of Small Wars*. They did not seem very small to me but they involved small military forces. This book changed my opinion about warfare and I have been an advocate of professional armies ever since.

"Read it," the colonel said, "read it, but keep your views to yourself."

Pour Another One, Tolik

This story began long ago. I was nine and it was early spring in Astrakhan. I returned home at about three in the afternoon and our housekeeper, Dusia, provided me with some food. I skimmed through my homework in an hour, got ready quickly and left the house. My parents were at work and would not be home until a couple of hours later.

As a rule, no one in my family was interested in what I got up to in my spare time; in fact they were unaware I had any. My parents regarded my success in mathematics as the only thing worth bothering about, everything else was just a trifling matter in their opinion and I would have to handle it myself; they worked so much they hardly ever saw me. I was not bothered by this because I really valued my freedom. That afternoon I had my own plans, I was going to play standard hockey with a ball with my friends. Canadian-style ice hockey was not something we knew about in those days.

I set off from home wearing a short overcoat and a fur cap, with my ears tucked in. My shoes with skates were laced together and slung over my shoulder, and my feet were in socks that had once been white, and plunged in galoshes. I wore galoshes because they were easy to stick under my belt when I was putting on my skates. Skates, of course, were essential and we called them 'padded', probably because they were not narrow like those worn by figure skaters; they were hollow in the middle with a wide blade.

I wore all my clothes while we played because if I had left anything unattended it would have been stolen immediately. Those were the rules we lived by. I had once put my cap on the chair next to me in the school library and when I looked up from my book it had gone. I had to go home, cap-less, through minus twenty degrees of frost, with my head swaddled in a scarf. I was so cold I had almost flown home.

Now I headed for the nearest tributary of the Volga, called the Kutum. It was quite a large river, about two hundred metres wide, and frozen over, but the temperature was not too cold because it was the beginning of March. There were occasional thaws, so the ice near the bank was weak, but towards the middle of the river it was firm enough to skate on. Swapping my footwear, I slithered on to the ice from the dangerously steep bank and carefully navigated to a safer area. The other boys were already waiting for me. We split up into teams, marked out the goals, and the game began.

We enthusiastically chased the ball around for two hours before the group gradually began to drift homewards. I had no idea what time it was because I did not wear a watch then, but it was dark and I sensed it was about seven in the evening. It was cold and dark on the river and was becoming increasingly deserted. I was also planning to go home but decided to go ashore at a more convenient, more level place, so I swiftly skated one hundred metres down the river and headed for the shore, which lay darkly in the distance. I was only twenty metres away when the ice suddenly gave way beneath me and I plunged into the icy water. Either the ice here was weak or in the darkness I had blundered into an ice hole where the local women did their laundry.

"Help," I yelled at the top of my boyish voice. "Aaaaaaaaa," I yelled again and again.

Someone must have heard me because I heard loud swearing and imprecations being hurled at my mother. I saw the dark figure of a man attempting to traverse the ice, which cracked and broke beneath him. He swore again as he lay on his stomach and wriggled towards me. The rim of the ice hole kept slipping out of my grasp but I gripped it with my remaining strength. At last the man was close enough to grab my collar and haul me on to the ice so we could crawl to the riverbank. When I was standing on solid ground and soaked to the skin, I looked at my saviour. He was wearing a dark jacket and trousers, his face was obscured by the darkness, he had a seedy appearance and his age was unclear.

There were three of them at the side of the river, they were homeless, although back then we called them tramps. They were just pouring a glass for each of them when had I turned up with my problem.

"Lad," one of them said, "piss off. We haven't even wet our whistles yet and Tolik is drenched."

Still wearing my skates, I sprinted home as quickly as I could. I had lost my galoshes in the water and my wet clothes were starting to freeze, but while I was running I warmed up a little.

My parents had not yet arrived home, I later found out they had visited someone straight after work, and Dusia was bustling around the kitchen and did not bother me. I threw off my wet clothes and put on some dry ones before carrying the soaked garments into the yard and hanging them on the clothesline. It was so cold that when I fetched them in at bedtime they were frozen, but almost dry. I was fortunate not to even catch a cold; I think the adrenalin rush I had experienced helped to prevent this. Nearly drowning had clearly scared the life out of me.

I felt a profound sense of obligation to my homeless rescuer. Someone I did not know had saved my life. The next day, when I returned from school, I went straight to the dresser on which my piggy bank stood. I had been regularly filling it with the small change left over from my breakfasts and that I had occasionally received from my parents. They were pleased with this thriftiness and thought it would be useful later in life. My official version was that I was saving for a penknife, but that was not how I intended to use the money now. I took the piggy bank, put it in a dish and smashed it with a hammer. I counted the change and found there were thirty pre-reform roubles. My mother had to work as a school teacher for a whole month to earn seven hundred roubles. I knew that a bottle of *Suchka* vodka, with a yellow sticker on the label, cost twenty-one roubles and fifty kopecks.

I gathered up the money, got dressed and went back to the scene of the previous day's drama. There was no one there so I returned the next evening and again the next day and evening. I continued to return until, finally, there came a day when I heard the familiar words, "Pour it out, Tolik." I drew closer and saw it was him.

"Hey, aren't you the one who pulled me out of the water?" I asked.

"Is it you?" he slurred drunkenly. Obviously they had already downed a few.

"Here it is guy," I said, handing him my treasure, "there's about thirty roubles. I want you to have this because I spoiled your party."

He stared blankly at the money and his face flushed with anger. "Get lost boy," he said, "I didn't slither out there for cash. And where's the money from? Did you steal it from your mother?"

"I didn't steal anything, I broke open my piggy bank."

"Tolik, what are you up to?" his drinking companions asked, alarmed by the fact the money might be taken away, "that's enough to fill our bellies? Take it, have you lost your mind?"

Tolik hesitated, but the temptation was too great. "Well, great, but I won't take your money," he said at last, "you'll have to go into the shop yourself."

"Okay," I said, and ran to the shop. I gave the shop worker some pathetic tale about my alcoholic rascal of a father and my poor mother who urgently needed help. I had fortunately seen similar scenario in the families of many of my school friends. *Forgive me, my poor deceased father, you didn't need this.* The shop worker clearly also had experience in this area and sold me the vodka without any questions.

I returned to Tolik and his friends.

"Look," said one of them, "he's so small and yet he's a man. Maybe you'd like to have a drink with us?"

"Don't bother the lad," said Tolik, "best just pour it out."

It was not long before they were all very drunk. His drinking companions disappeared, but Tolik had drunk so much he did not move and kept nodding off. I was worried he might freeze to death. I realised that the amount of vodka he had drunk meant the evening could end badly for my saviour so I asked him to lean on me and guided him to the sawmill in the yard of our residential block. I laid him down comfortably on a large pile of fragrant sawdust. In the morning the chief tree feller, a one-legged disabled war veteran called Vasia, showed up. I had a trusting relationship with him and explained to him why there was a tramp in his mill.

"OK," he said, "he can stay here, but it won't be for too long." Vasia had a terrific understanding of people.

Tolik stayed on and began to help him with the work for a modest fee in the form of alcohol and food. He guarded the sawmill and occasionally substituted for Vasia in the relationships with local ladies. At that time only ten years had passed since the war and there was a shortage of men.

Two months passed in this manner. In April I was sick and had to take two weeks off school. When I was well enough to return I had to catch up with my lessons, so after school I would arrange myself on a workbench in the sawmill. It was more fun there than at home, which was empty. Tolik and Vasia would have a drink and a bite to eat, and Vasia would relax while having a smoke. Tolik approached me to watch how I did my homework and, unexpectedly, began to explain the material to me and corrected a few mistakes, but so clearly that

I understood what he had done. I was taken aback, I would never have expected this from him.

One week later Tolik was gone. Vasia knew what he was talking about, it really had not been a long time. I never saw Tolik in Astrakhan again. Rumour had it that he had travelled south to warmer climes. Subsequently, Vasia told me Tolik's story. Before the war he worked as a teacher in a village school and had been married with a child. When the war came he was on the front, his unit retreated and he was captured and released, then assigned to a punishment battalion, wounded and demobilised. While he was away his home had been bombed and his family were killed. After that he had taken to drink, started stealing and been sentenced to a prison camp. Now he lived as a tramp, a rolling stone, and a free man. There were many who had suffered a similar destiny all around us. Tolik was lucky, at least he was still alive - And I never forgot that I was alive too, thanks to him.

The story is not yet finished. Long ago, life taught me that that it contains no incomplete stories, you just have to wait a while.

I studied, completed my studies at school and entered an educational institute in Odesa. During my third year, in October 1965, I signed up for a Sunday trip to Chisinau, along with my friends. It was a form of shopping we had back then when, in the Soviet Union, supplies to the retail network were under strict central control, there was almost nothing on the shelves of the shops in Odesa and everything was bought very expensively on the market. Chisinau, although smaller than Odesa, was the capital of the Moldova Soviet Republic and therefore was in a higher supply category. It was occasionally possible to buy things in the shops at prices fixed by the state there. I was living on seventy-five post reform roubles each month, which my parents sent me. My small earnings on the side did not really count, so this parental stipend was vital for me to be able to buy anything.

We travelled merrily in the *PAZyk*, the soviet charabanc, singing and drinking. The ancient chronicler Nestor was right when he said, "The pleasures of Rus are drinking and merrymaking." These are pretty much the same words with which Prince Volodymyr supposedly argued for Rus to adopt Christianity rather than Islam.

We arrived in Chisinau, did some shopping and headed back. Everyone wanted a bit more fun so we stopped off in a Moldavian village to ask where we could buy some wine. We were directed towards a respectable looking house from which a fat, moustached Moldavian emerged and, haggling a little, sold us a bucket of home-brew wine.

"Ivan," he yelled, "pour 'em a bucket."

An old man with the look of a heavy drinker appeared and something stirred within me. "Tolik is it you?" I asked, stunned. "It's me, Boris, you pulled me from the water in Astrakhan." I looked into his dulled eyes, but he did not recognise me or remember anything.

It was so obviously Tolik so I approached the boss. "Has he worked for you for a long time?"

"Yes, two years," he replied, "he turned up here and remembered nothing of his past and had no documents. The police had a look at him and then just left him. I took him in. He works well and eats almost nothing; he just drinks."

I tried to meet Tolik's eyes again, but he did not react.

"What do you call him?" I asked the Moldavian peasant.

"Ivan. Is that right?"

"Tolik," I replied, "they call him Tolik."

My friend and I left and Tolik disappeared from my life again. Ten years later, in 1975, I participated in the design and construction of the pipeline system which supplied western European countries with Russian gas. One of the areas where I supervised construction was in Moldova, very close to the village where I had seen Tolik. I was in a car one day and headed there, where I found the same respectable house. The owner had not changed much, only his moustache had turned white.

"Do you remember a man you called Ivan, who worked for you?" I asked.

"Yes," he replied, "he died a year after you called by."

"What did he die of?"

"I don't know. I think he was just tired of living," came the reply.

"Do you remember anything else?"

"He told me something about himself, mentioned a few names, but, sorry, I don't remember. It was a long time ago."

"Where is he buried?"

"The grave hasn't survived, there was no one to look after it."

The tale was over. I had seen only a small part of the drama of Tolik's life, but for me this crossing of our paths was hugely significant, perhaps decisive for my destiny. I thought about it for a long time until time itself began to dull my memories. So now I record this story and again reflect on these events and how this tale is typical of all of us; of the many people whose destinies are broken by wars, cataclysms, monstrous injustices … all of which always arise on the soil where we live and die. How many people have these events cast to the side-lines of life? How many have fallen under the blows of destiny?

Around the world people treat the homeless differently, and in many places they either look down on them or abuse them; in others they help them out as best they can. As the bible says:

Judge not, that ye be not judged. For with what judgment ye judge, ye shall be judged: and with what measure ye mete, it shall be measured to you again. (Mathew 7 1:2)

And that seems the right place to end this tale.

Lala, or the Gypsy's Curse

Long, long ago, on a day in March, when I was in the tenth grade, a new girl was introduced to our class; her brilliantly brunette hair and black, shining eyes gave her a very distinctive appearance. She wore a bright, multi-coloured skirt and plush jacket, and her red scarf gleamed against the darkness of her tresses. She was a Gypsy and had come from the large Gypsy encampment located on the outskirts of the city. She looked painfully askance at the grey provincial background of Astrakhan.

She was older than the rest of the class, I was sixteen and she was about eighteen; a grown woman as far as I was concerned. Her name was Lala and I noticed her immediately, but she paid me no attention and it seemed she even disliked me. She only possessed the most minimal academic knowledge, even though she was pretty smart, daring and had a sharp tongue, and me helping her with her studies was the background to how we got acquainted. Once I had explained something that puzzled her, I was emboldened and went to her home. Her family lived in rented apartments in private housing, which had large courtyards where they pitched their tents and tethered their horses. I understood they were waiting for warmer weather before they would move on.

Unfortunately, their camp was on the turf of one of the city's gangs called The Kosinskye, or Sandbar boys (from the word 'kosa' or spit), and they let no one else venture on to their territory; especially not near their women. My appearance with Lala caused quite a stir: although Lala could not be considered their woman, my visits were a breach of the order on their territory and their leader, Pasha, nicknamed 'The Goat', who was the same age as me, let me know in no uncertain terms that he would have to stick it to me because I had blundered there, as he spat through his metal teeth.

"Where should I have 'blundered'?" I asked indignantly. "How is she to get home? What are you, an occupier who will not let anyone pass through your territory? Do you want to ravish her yourselves?"

"Nah," said Pasha, "she isn't one of our lot. Mess with this Gypsy and they'll tear your bollocks off." He made a decision which prevented any altercation. "Well, carry on, don't hang around our territory, just walk her home and back. Okay?"

"Okay," I replied and received 'diplomatic immunity'.

We walked mostly along the Volga and by mid-April both the weather and our relationship had warmed up. We went pretty far, far enough in certain ways, after all Lala was an adult. Well, not quite, but…

I was unsure how her relatives would react to our meetings, but everything seemed to be calm. I had never seen her father and was not even sure if he was alive or still lived with them, but her mother, a strapping, fat Gypsy woman, paid no more attention to me than any of the other young men in the camp. The elder of their group was a severe looking, bearded Roma, about fifty years old; he asked my name then paid me no more heed.

Was it love between Lala and me? I am not certain if the emotion was fully formed; it was probably just an interest that was not strong enough to flower into love. The May holiday approached and at the end of May I graduated from school and began to prepare thoroughly for entering technical college. One evening I asked Lala what she was going to do when she left school.

"I don't know yet," she said chirpily, "probably get married. The chief has already negotiating my wedding."

"What, don't you even know who?"

"Why should I know?" she said, and changed the topic.

One week later when I met her she was really upset. "We're leaving in a week and I'll be married in a fortnight. The dowry is already sorted."

"But you won't finish school," I protested.

"Well, I've been going to the tenth grade for three years anyway," she said as tears glittered in her eyes.

My blood boiled with all of youth's hyperbolic passion, but what could I offer her; I was a teenager who still attended school. I walked her home and the group's elder reacted to me for the first time. "Boris, you must come here no more," he said, "I forbid it. And watch out or you'll have problems."

Despite his warning, I could not resist my feelings and returned the next day. I met her mother this time and it was a much more raucous encounter. She stuck her hands on her hips and totally blocked the doorway with her massive frame. It is probably better not to spell it out in detail, I had never heard language like it before or since. She cursed me so that everything in my life would wither and fall, so I would have neither a recess in which to seek refuge, nor a covering for my head. So that I would have neither good fortune nor happiness, neither women nor money. I failed to understand some of the words, but it all sounded pretty threatening. Lala was behind me because I had escorted her from school and she dragged me away by the arm until we were at a safe distance. We reached the bank of the Volga, which was thickly overgrown with scrub, after a while.

"Boris," she said, "don't be afraid. Maybe we don't see each other for a while, but I will cast a spell now. Listen."

We went deeper into the bushes. Suddenly she closed her eyes and began speaking one, very long, sentence in a strange language. Then, opening her eyes, she kissed me on the lips and turned away. "I'm going now," she said, "don't follow me."

"What was it you said?"

"It's an ancient spell, it will protect you from curses and the evil eye until we meet again."

38

"And will we meet again?"

"Of course, it is certain."

Lala turned and disappeared. She did not appear at school the following day nor the day after that. On the third day I could contain myself no longer and went to the camp. I could see they had already gone, but the landlord confirmed it, "They've upped sticks," he said.

"Where've they gone?" I asked.

"Who knows, Gypsies drift like wind through a field."

The following day I refused to go to school and my parents were concerned, so called a doctor who found nothing wrong with me. I was in a strange condition of both physical and mental numbness which passed after a couple of days and I managed to pull myself together and get back into my studies. My parents still knew nothing about my encounter and saga with Lala and I never said anything. I finished tenth grade, passed the examination, received a maturation certificate and went to college in Odesa.

Three years later I finished the third year of my course; it was May 1966. After the last lecture I had lunch at the 'Kiev' restaurant on Grecheska Square, which operated as a diner during daylight hours, and decide to take a stroll before doing some sports training. I reached Soborna Square where I sat and smoked a cigarette. I looked around and saw many Gypsies, more precisely Gypsy women, in the park. They scurried swiftly along the pathways, accosting passers-by and offering to tell their fortunes if their palms were crossed with silver. There was only one man among them, he was standing to one side and overseeing their labours.

"I'll tell your fortune my precious," I heard someone say in a singing voice. A young Gypsy girl sat next to me on the bench and rearranged her gaudy skirt. Then she looked at me and in an unexpectedly normal voice asked, "Boris, is it you? It's me, Elvira."

When I was friends with Lala, Elvira had been thirteen and used to pass notes between us when we were arranging a rendezvous. She was sixteen now and a beautiful girl. "Yes, it's me."

"You?" her eyes widened, as if she had seen something unusual. She rose suddenly and shouted something at her clan. The square was empty in a moment. The Gypsies bunched together in a gaudily coloured mass and swiftly departed.

I sat there uncomprehendingly. I had not even had time to ask about Lala, about the spell or if we were destined to meet again. I shook my head. Oh well, I was in a spin again and thought about how daft those spells were as I remembered them. But Lala … I went through that day in a daze.

Life continued in its own merry way. So much and so many different things happen in this life. However, in some nook of my memory was a closet with a massive lock on the door; it guarded that secret question, what happened?

As I have said previously, I reached the conclusion that all of life's stories are eventually concluded; however, the finale to my saga with Lala would not be completed until sixteen years later, in 1982, during a business trip to the city of Nevinnomysk, Stavropol territory. The institute where I worked had developed a plan for renovating the gas pipeline that linked to a local chemical plant there.

I alighted quickly from the train at Nevinnomysk on the North Caucasus line because I was only staying for two to three days so had very little luggage. I strode towards the station building and the city, but as I approached the building I encountered a middle-aged Gypsy woman sitting on the platform. "Boris," she said softly as I passed, "it's me, Elvira."

I looked at her. Judging by her appearance, you would have thought she was forty-five. I made a quick mental calculation and realised she must be about thirty-two, but she looked as though life had not been kind to her. "Elvira," I said,

40

halting beside her, "what's up with Lala? Don't run off, answer me. And where are you camped?"

She rose and spoke rapidly again, "Lala is no more, she died giving birth. Her daughter, also called Lala, survived, she is over there with her dad." She pointed to the end of the platform. A tall, young Gypsy woman in a colourful skirt and plush jacket with a red scarf in her black hair stood with her back towards me. An elderly man in a wide, felt hat, with a grey beard stood near her.

"Why do you run off all the time?" I asked Elvira.

"We can't talk with you, for you are cursed," said Elvira. "Only she can."

Elvira fled, looking downward and away from me. I headed for the end of the platform as I considered whether my childhood affections could bring new life to my jaded existence. No, I thought, no perhaps not. "Lala," I called. She turned. It was her, Lala, in the fullness of her beauty and youth at eighteen; jet black hair and dark, shining eyes. We were destined to meet and we had met. I looked into her eyes and, though it was a warm spring day, I shivered. I jerked involuntarily. We had met and the curse was lifted. She smiled, breaking the spell. I crossed her palm with silver, all the change I found in my pocket, and left.

I met Elvira again by the station building. "Why haven't you fled?" I asked her.

"There is no need for me to flee now," she smiled, "it's okay for us to talk. Do you want me to tell your fortune?"

"Don't," I said, "for all of my future has already happened."

We parted, each of us going about their own work. *Farewell Lala, I don't think we will see each other again in this life.*

Mamba, or the Chief's Daughter

I met a woman from Africa, who was studying at Odesa University on a cultural exchange programme, during my fourth year at college. I was studying at the communications institute and our meeting took place quite by chance when we both accompanied friends to a dance at the university. It was spring and hormonal feelings raged in the breasts of us young men, despite the poor victuals that sustained us. I plucked up the courage to ask her to join me in a dance and afterwards we roamed the Langeron area of Odesa[1]. She was slim with a very sexy look and matching behaviour; her curves were in all the right places and she was proud of her full, feminine figure. Her liberal approach to relations manifested itself on that first night when we became friends, which was quite startling for a man from the Soviet Union.

I began to visit her, sometimes alone and sometimes with friends, at her hostel. There were many beauties there, so all our group found a date. We bribed one of the doorwomen, an old Odesa madam, and arranged our visits to coincide with her shifts.

My girl was from Dahomey and was one of the numerous members of the Yoruba tribe. When I knew her better she told me that she was the daughter of a tribal chief; most interestingly she was a Mamba, a sorceress in the voodoo cult, along with all the women in her family. My friends and I took this in our stride and we all called her Mamba after that, particularly because we all struggled to pronounce her real name. She did not seem to mind and so became Mamba for us.

To say she was attractive does not do her beauty justice. She was fiendishly, fiendishly alluring, but walking around Odesa with a woman from Africa was dangerous in those days. The majority of people in the port city would not approve, so we usually went around in a group. I had three friends who

42

were like me, tearaways, and always out for adventure. We had one shared good quality, we were diligent students, but a mass of other, to put it mildly, appalling, attributes. We drank, caroused, and stuck our noses in where they were not wanted … we regularly brawled with other young men, then made it up, then brawled again. When I remember this period I think that young people have to burn with life and to cut lose. It is only really bad if you start carrying on like that as an adult. So, naturally, every age has its own appropriate behaviour.

We hung out and had a good time for a while until I suddenly discovered that Mamba had, quietly but openly, initiated close relationships with all our gang. It was a startling revelation and initially I was unsure how to react. Finally, I decided to talk about it. I asked my friends if they had been involved with her and they confirmed that they had. I asked Mamba about the matter and she told me that she considered this to be normal. It was the most humdrum affair in her tribe. Any girl aged thirteen and above could go to any man, sometimes even after marriage. Indeed, for a Mamba, as a sorceress, it was a sacred duty. "Your friends are your tribe, so it's okay," she told me.

What else could I do but accept this explanation? At least I could manage that for a while before the summer holidays. Then, I thought to myself, we would sort it out.

The second semester and exams were approaching and it was essential that I allocated some of my precious time for studying. This distressed Mamba and she reproached us occasionally. She did not need to study really; her country was continuously afflicted by military coups and radical changes of political course. During this period it was next in line on the 'socialist path of development'. She was, therefore, very highly esteemed by the soviets; she did not have to speak at oral exams and tests, and never got anything less than a good grade four. On the basis of her own experience, she thought studying was a breeze and was surprised by our efforts. She probably felt in her soul that the Yoruba were far smarter than the local youths.

One evening something odd happened when I was walking home from the institute. My college was situated in Cheliuskintsev Street and at that time I was living with some distant relatives in a basement apartment on Chkalova Street (now Velyka Arnautska Street), I was almost home when I met a neighbour's boy with a dog; his father had worked as a butcher at Privoz, so he was one of the local aristocracy. I was a professor's son, but I still lived in a basement, so he treated me with brazen contempt. I would have given him a pasting straight away but his dog, a Great Dane, was pretty terrifying. More significantly, it took an immediate dislike to me, barked and lunged towards me. I had only seen him on a lead before and now he was charging off on his own. His owner was by his side smoking and seemed oblivious to the massive dog with a muffled growl rushing at me.

Thoughts swirled swiftly through my head and I recollected everything I had ever read about dogs attacking humans and other animals. Rapidly sifting through all this, I settled on a somewhat risky option; I would grab the dog's lower jaw when he opened his mouth to attack me and thus prevent him from holding me in his grip. I had read about this manoeuvre in a Jack London novel. It was not safe, of course, and I was unsure whether the writer had made it up. He probably never expected that someone would attempt this 'deadly' performance in real life. But I could not think of anything better to do in the circumstances.

The dog ran towards me, thrust his hind legs and opened his red maw. I struggled but somehow managed to grab his jaw and press down. His fangs slipped between my fingers and I avoided being injured. He tried to open his jaw, but did not have the leverage because I was gripping him so strongly. It was a stalemate; neither of us could break off this 'friendly'

44

hug. Eventually the dog broke his grip and shook his head with canine screams to show he disapproved of my behaviour. The owner also ran towards me and, seeing my hands were occupied, decided to give me a good talking to. In short, the dog and I were somehow uncoupled without either of us suffering too much damage.

The following day I told Mamba about my encounter and her response surprised me. "I can sort out this problem for you."

"How?" I asked in amazement.

"Every one of us corresponds to the image of an animal. Some of us are predators, such as the lion, leopard, and cheetah, while others are herbivores, like the antelope or buffalo. You, for example, are a predator, though you don't know it. I can make it so that any animal, such as a dog, will sense your real form and they won't want to engage with you."

It struck me as an amusing idea and I agreed to participate, but as the ritual began I must admit that I did not like it. She had bought a white cockerel at Privoz, which she decapitated, sprinkled some of its blood on her breast and drew a symbol on my right hand with its gore. She danced and sang something in her own tongue. We were on a deserted and unlit beach and my friends were on lookout duty so no one could hamper our ritual. Finally, she plunged into the sea and demanded that someone 'spoke' with her. I obliged.

"Well, from now onwards," she said, "if you want an animal to sense your true nature, point your right hand towards it and make horns by tucking in your first and fourth finger into your fist."

We accompanied her back to the hostel and I went home. The dog saw me from afar and ran strenuously towards me.

"Bite him, bite him," screamed its owner.

We'll put this magic to the test now, I thought without

much enthusiasm. When the dog had run ten metres I stuck out my right hand, made the required horns in its direction and yelled, "Back off beast." The spell had an amazing impact. The massive dog suddenly slammed on the brakes on all its four paws, then yelped, turned and scarpered, leaving his master gawping. I strode proudly to the entrance to my lowly basement apartment.

"How'd it go?" Mamba asked me a couple of days later when we met at her hostel.

"Okay," I said, a little embarrassed. I would have liked to check it again but the dog had not approached close enough after our last encounter.

Mamba sniffed in a contented manner and looked at me triumphantly.

One month later the course year finished, we went home and Mamba made the long trip back to Dahomey. The rest of us returned in September but she languished in Africa, where another coup had occurred. Dahomey had binned socialism and was now re-focusing on a pro-western vector, so Mamba lost her value in the eyes of the state. Perhaps she continued her studies at the Sorbonne or somewhere else. I will never know.

Weirdly enough, however, the ritual performed on the beach still has an effect. I have noticed that animals are scared of me, including dogs, horses, and even the denizens of zoos. Only cats are not scared, probably because they look down on us[2]; or maybe they see me as a relative. But no animal has any reason to be scared of me, I treat them well and have never hit them or even swung a limb menacingly at them. I was fond of horses, but now, when I sit in the saddle, my favourite mare's ears stick out and she trembles. She only calms down when we break into a trot, but if I halt her she becomes scared again.

My relationship with dogs is even worse. I was once walking through a car park with a friend when we saw a huge dog chained up in the distance. We were cool about it because he was a long way off, but it transpired the chain was attached to a ring which slid along a cable, and the cable ran across the whole of the car park. We realised this when we trod on it and disturbed the dog who swiftly ran up to us. He looked at my comrade and launched himself towards him, but he just yelped at me, like a puppy wagging his tail happily. My friend did not lose much; though his briefcase was firmly gripped between the dog's jaws.

So I knew the 'spell' worked, though over time the effect got weaker. For it to work fully now I needed to touch the animal. Recently I decided to test whether it still worked, even though forty-three years have passed since the ritual. I have a guard dog at home, a German Shepherd of noble lineage called Westus House Favour, or simply West; he has been with me since he was four months old and he is now seven years old. He can be incredibly frightening to strangers, but he is good with me; I treat him well and he looks after me too.

I fed him as usual and laid my right hand on his head; this huge dog, usually scared of nothing, put his ears back and trembled so violently that it made me feel cold too. "West, what's up with you?" I said, soothingly petting him on the shoulder with my left hand - it had to be the left of course…

"There are more things in heaven and earth, Horatio. Than are dreamed of in your philosophy."

[1] The coastal area of Odesa in the vicinity of the former summer residence of Count Louis Alexandre Andrault de Langeron, Count of Langeron, Marquis de la Coste, , Baron de Cougny. Between 1815 and 1823 he was mayor of Odesa and Governor of the area termed New Russia by the Tsarist regime.
[2] Winston Churchill once said, "I like pigs. Dogs look up to us. Cats look down on us. Pigs treat us as equals."

A Study Against the Backdrop of a Boxing Ring

A killer punch and the hefty man fell to the icy ground and almost landed on and crushed me; I was a slight, eleven year old boy at the time. He lay on his back and a state of blissful confusion was evident in his misty eyes, but it only took him a minute to recover.

"Wow, Semionich smacked him proper," yelled my contemporaries, who were fans, of these informal bouts. The wall of spectators, including me, had bent to allow for his fall, but the circle did not break.

"Smack him in the gut now."

Yet another fighter was felled and slowly came to, gasping frantically for air. Meanwhile, Semionich tackled the leader. The chief was a head taller than Semionich and twice as wide across the shoulders. In his ordinary life the chief was a foreman for a group of freight loaders. Things went sour for him now. He swung at his opponent and missed, swung again and hit nothing. Semionich retaliated and his blows landed like a sharpshooter's bullets on target. A left, a right, a hook to the head over the chief's guard and under it to the gut. The hulking foreman swayed, shook his head and flopped to sit on the ice. Everyone yelled.

It was the first time I had seen a boxing match. We lived in Astrakhan then and the summers were unbearable, so my parents, who were teachers, used their long mid-term break to take me and my little brother somewhere more fit for human life. Sometimes they would take us to my birthplace, Odesa, and occasionally we went to resorts in Crimea and the Caucasus. The only stipulation was that we were near the sea. While running, swimming and bathing I got into the shape I would exploit mercilessly for the rest of my life. I thank my parents for that. But, as I think about it now, I remember one funny episode.

In 1963, I sat my first exam, mathematics, at the Odesa Institute of Electro-technological Communications. The other candidates and I entered the hall and sat at the desks. The tasks we could choose were chalked on the board, but were still covered in sheets of white paper so we would not need to make our selection until the invigilators peeled off the paper.

All my senses were heightened; I could see, hear and feel everything as if through an amplifier or a magnifying glass. The window offered me a view of lush vegetation. I heard very clearly and loudly the words, "By the sea, the blue sea, where seagulls call in the vastness of the sky…" It was someone's tape recorder. On the desk where I was sitting someone had scrawled in ink, *spring has passed, summer has come, thank the Party for that.* At this moment of massive stress I took out my pen and added to the inscription, *summer didn't pass too badly, dear parents, thanks to you.*

"What's that?" the invigilator asked. I had not noticed him behind me.

"So you can only write in praise of the Party?" I retorted in outrage.

Before he could reply the options were revealed and silence reigned; I did not have time to worry about them and managed to solve all the proposed tasks mentally at first glance. Then two undergraduates came in and moved the board to reveal another option, which I also quickly decided I would like to pick.

My parents' endeavours in preparing me for this since I was five years old paid off, I finished mathematical school and won the Astrakhan Maths Olympiad. Then, in 1963, I won the All Soviet Mathematical Physics Olympiad, so I was extremely familiar with elementary mathematics. It was just awkward that I did not like the subject, or rather it was not my vocation.

I wrote my answer to the first question, then the second, then, for some diversion, the third, then after time to relax, the fourth. I wrote it all up and handed it to the invigilator in about an hour and a half. After this cakewalk I had a hard time in the second exam, oral mathematics. I felt the examiners had it in for me and if it was not for my youthful insolence (I demanded public access to the materials of the exam committee) it would have ended badly for me.

But let's go back to the boxers and the ice. Yes, summer was hard in Astrakhan, but winter was okay. The Volga and its tributaries, the Kutum and Kanava rivers, froze. We cleared the ice and sorted out skating rinks on their surfaces. We played hockey and raced on our skates until evening. Fights were arranged, with strong healthy men lining up on opposing walls to batter each other. It took a long time to set them up. People would start arriving, usually in sheepskin coats; ladies, the fiancés and wives, wore boots. We welcomed them, gave them a glass or two of something to drink and the competitors threw down their coats. It was advantageous to be a child arranging the bouts and it was considered an honour. I participated a couple of times and ended up battling some real pile drivers, but I did not go far because it was painful to be skinny in these affrays.

The adults began by an exchange of menacing words, they mocked each other and only then slowly began to brawl. Once in full swing they would exchange full force, bare-knuckle blows. Knuckle dusters were banned. Dodging was beneath anyone's dignity and the fight continued until the first blood was drawn, until the contestants were falling but managing to stay upright, or until one of us was battered out of the ring that had been marked out. It would have been easy to step into a weak spot in the ice if anyone ventured too far. We would wash the blood down an ice hole and leap on to the wide shoulders of those downed in the battle. We would embrace our martial companions and go somewhere else to have a bit of fun.

Ice boxing was popular at that time and it would have

been great if it were not for a newcomer turning up. Semionich was about forty and sturdy, but not tall. He did not immediately join in the fights, but he worked as a boxing trainer in the 'labour reserves'. No one came to train with him because the local men felt it was pointless. "We're okay without boxing, anyone who likes it can, we'll bash their face in," they said.

So, Semionich decided to reason with these sceptics by offering a practical example. His demonstrations were superb and his opponents had no chance. It worked and people began to turn up for his sessions. Two years later and Astrakhan shone like a beacon in the country's boxing rings. Semionich had also grown in stature and was given an apartment and the fancy title of 'Honoured Coach'. When I was twelve, without my parents' knowledge, I was one of his first pupils. I asked him to sign me up for his classes, but he was skeptical. "You're so lanky. It wouldn't hurt to sort that out first. Get in shape and we'll see."

Nevertheless, I turned up to every session and eventually he gave in and admitted me. I loved it, it made me feel good. When I saw spectators, sensed them, I felt euphoric and trained incessantly. It was such a contrast for me, someone who was preparing for a science career and for whom the real world existed in books.

After a couple of months my parents found out what I was taking part in and although they were alarmed at first, they eventually accepted the idea. I think the trainer said something not very flattering about my physique to them, but they convinced themselves that it would be a brief phase for me.

I was not allowed to spar for my first year, but I trained hard and the day came when I could enter the ring. I had a real rating, as they said then, as a fighter. There were three rounds of two minutes each. I was in a blue shirt and shorts and blue sneakers, and standing, of course, in the blue corner. My opponent was in the opposite corner, wearing red. I had never seen him before. I heard the gong and the fight flared up.

I won my first fight with surprising ease and swiftness and still remember it well. No one rooted for me at the ringside and there was nowhere to retreat. The ring, with its four roped-off sides, was a real symbol of the struggles of life. I realised part of the truth of existence: If you want to win life's battles, burn your bridges behind you. That eliminates the possibility of retreat. Many years passed before I understood the second part of the truth. If you want to win the war, keep your bridges and retreat tactically if you need to, but be unstoppable in realising your ultimate goal.

My head was dizzy with my first successes. I excelled among the first ranks of boxing youth for three years and shone among my peers, until the day I met a really strong boxer and was brought down to earth with a bump. I knew if I wanted to continue I would have to begin treating boxing much more seriously.

Times changed and life went on. Along with boxing, my time was taken up with study, books and girls; I needed to get ready for college. Everything had to be done all at once and I tried as hard as I could. I felt then that life was an off-road ride over rough terrain and that my goal was an unattainable distant star. I felt as if the light of distant, celestial objects warmed me. Indeed their radiance warms me still.

A new phase in my boxing life began when I entered college. The sports hall at the Institute of Communication was in an old German church, which had a high, oh so high, roof. Boxers trained in one corner, classical wrestlers in another, and gymnasts and acrobats in the middle. The wrestlers were sturdy young men and we were skinny, so they started to pick on us. We all had enough pride and both sides challenged each other to a fight, which at first seemed as if it was going to be a lawless brawl. The wrestlers put on gloves to box us and we dispatched them effortlessly. Then they took them off and we kept on our gloves and had no chance. Then we took off our gloves and we found that we were evenly matched. We began to conclude our training with these freestyle fights. Word got around the city and soon spectators began to arrive; these were our peers. The bouts were traumatic and fun despite an occasional broken nose or twisted ear.

I was called to the Komsomol committee once and asked to explain my appearance and behaviour. Only the evidence of my coach let me survive that ordeal unscathed. It transpired I had gallantly defended the institute's colours and raised the prestige of soviet sports (these words are taken verbatim from his report). The committee included some attractive girls and I often turned up; they did not know how to get rid of me by then. We were wasters in those unforgettable days.

My parents lived in Simferopol while I studied in Odesa and I had total freedom. I would study or enjoy myself as I pleased and only had myself to answer to; it was a risky but useful experience for life. I attended the institute, had lunch, then trained in the sports hall before having a ball. It was like that day after day. Soon the boxing ring was opened at the weekends. We did not fight for money, we battled for honour and food; if you took part, you received coupons that could be swapped for free sour cream and butter. Imagine how much I gorged myself on the stuff. Enough to last a lifetime. I refrain from indulging in any such rich food now.

During that period in my life, against the backdrop of the boxing ring, I experienced many interesting things; I had some great friends, fights with my peers, and romances with some of the ladies among them. Many of the future members of the émigré Bohemia, whose work we later listened to on cassettes, and then saw on TV, lived in Odesa at that time. They were so young.

Like most students, I never had enough money and earned it however I could. Of course my parents sent money, though they did not have much to spare; I was no exception, they had to economise with me too. I did odd jobs to supplement my income: hauling railway carriages to the commercial station, dragging the finished product to the winery, acting as an extra in the theatre and at the film studio, teaching courses for external students and submitting them for exam classes in school maths, and even standing in for them in maths Olympiads. This was not an exhaustive list of my exploits back then, however, it was at that time that I read a translation of a 19th Century Spanish Epigram:

He who does not have a true friend at fifteen years old
And twenty languid beauties
And thirty massive debts
And provision till he's forty
And fifty somethings worth of money
He's playing the fool whatever
He's a decent slacker.

I read it then, but it is only now that I realise what it means after so much time has passed. There is indeed 'nothing new under the sun'. Everything ends eventually, my time at college finished and ahead of me lay a period in the army. Being a young man in full possession of his faculties I wondered, while I was still at college, if I would see this time through rose-coloured spectacles. Surely not, I thought, everything up in the air, always without money, chaotic, an unsystematic lifestyle… That will never look good from any distance. I was mistaken. I very rarely remember the poverty and craziness. Now I only recollect the youth, health, the freshness of it all, the new sensations, the joy I gleaned from my achievements and my expectations of a future, which I knew would have to be terrific.

The army added many new things to my sporting life. The officers were young; I served as an officer after graduating from the institute's military faculty, and performing in competitions was mandatory. Everyone trained, so we were evenly matched. Officers were not involved in boxing, they looked after their health, I was the only officer in our garrison's boxing team. I did not train much, but I used my previous experience and from time to time won various bouts.

My first serious breakthrough came in the Odesa military district championships where I won three fights and met an old acquaintance from Odesa. He was just like me but had studied in a different institute where there was no military faculty, so had joined the army as a private and ended up in the sports squad. He trained and did not touch a drop of alcohol, just like a proper athlete.

Our tally of victories in our bouts against each other in Odesa was equal. However, the situation was different now for both of us. He was better prepared than I was, but I had no intention of loosing so the bout was tough. Neither of us gave way, we met in the middle of the ring and, forgetting about the fence, slugged each other until one of us fell; then slugged it out again until the other fell. And so on until the final bell. He won, but the way we had fought prompted one of the judges, who was my also my friend, to ask, "Was there something personal about that fight? Why did you turn the ring into an abattoir?"

"No," I replied, "neither of us wanted to give in?"

In those days there was quite a harsh custom in Odesa's sporting circles. If a fighter did not agree with the judges' decision he could compel a rematch on the same day, after the tournament, in the locker room. The ring would be improvised from those low benches found in changing rooms and there would be no break in the fight until one of the opponents was knocked out. It was impossible to back out of this challenge without losing face and I had to participate on two occasions which are best forgotten. Youth is harsh and uncompromising, but also beautiful, but the idea of a rematch did not occur to me after this fight, I was totally shattered.

That was the beginning of the end of my boxing career. Although I trained for another three years while I was still in the army and afterwards, it was clear this chapter of my life was over. So, I turned the page at twenty-six years old with a heavy heart. I did not stop participating in sports and I still do, even more than I need to, but other interests took over my life; these are stories for another time. Boxing had played a role in my life; without it I would be a different, perhaps better person, but not the human being I am now.

One of my favourite writers, Rudyard Kipling, once said:

Two things greater than all things are,
The first is Love, and the second War.
And since we know not how War may prove,
Heart of my heart, let us talk of Love!

I decided that the time of war had passed and the time of love had come. How wrong I was. The fundamental battles of my life yet lay ahead of me.

The bell rang for the end of the fight and I headed for my corner, panting. I was in my prime, attending the best university in the city of Odesa, in my first year at the institute of communications, and was boxing as a middleweight. There were only three, three minute rounds, so I wondered why was I so shattered, but maybe it was because this was the final. I took off my gloves and was preparing to unwrap the bandages on my hands when the referee called us into the middle of the ring.

I had lost on points but this was not a devastating loss for me; it was the first time I had participated in this type of match, so my conception of boxing had not yet matured. My opponent was twenty-five and studying for a higher degree in sport. I still had time. That was how I consoled myself, but something still troubled me. I had been involved in boxing since I was twelve and had attended a specialist sports school. I had acquired a lot of experience there as a sparring partner at the gym and during teenage fights in the break-times, and knew that I could always enhance my skills as a fighter. I considered what I could add to my game now, then I remembered; Jack London mentioned the Marquis of Queensbury rules in *The Abysmal Brute*. The rules had been published in 1867. A bout had lasted for twenty-four rounds then; before that there had not been any time limit. Professional fighters could now last up to fifteen rounds. And I was shattered after three…

These thoughts troubled me while I showered after the match. I got changed and went home to the basement flat where I lived with my distant relatives, Auntie Tsila and Uncle Iliushi. Those reflections, weirdly enough, did not leave me on the following day and I wondered if this was because my pride was still badly wounded.

During a maths lecture an interesting idea popped into my head; I should try to organise a long bout and put myself to the test. I made this suggestion to our coach when I attended a training session later that day. For some reason he was not surprised, "You know Boris," he said, "guys occasionally make these suggestions to me. They're young, hot blooded and have lots of energy without an outlet. But do not think it is easy, there has to be a particular mood for such a fight to take place; people rarely try it more than once, but let's give it a try. Warm up and climb into the ring, work on one round each with all the guys and say when you get tired." He looked at me and added, drawing out the words, "Don't strain… and watch yourself in the ring."

I did not strain myself, all my opponents were from the club and I had asked for this bout. I tried to go at a steady pace, work on counter punching in the middle of the ring, and avoid the corners and ropes. I kept moving sometimes when I was counter-attacking. Gradually I settled into the fight and began breathing evenly. The agitation had faded and I was focussed. This was perhaps better than the traditional three round amateur fight. In those short bouts a boxer bustles around, trying to show his best, and that tires him out. Above all he knows he needs to give it everything in three rounds and will be tired, but if he can just go beyond those determined boundaries by staging a long fight, he can determine the rules himself.

Interestingly, I did not particularly need breaks between the rounds; in fact I did not sit down in the minutes between the bell ringing. The fight continued and different young men came into the ring, boxed, left and were replaced. I kept watch over my feelings. Well, okay, I thought about how long I could maintain the state of equilibrium as the world around became blurred and out of focus, which was an unusual and new sensation, but, by contrast, I saw the ring and my opponents as if through a magnifying glass. Time had also shifted gear and was unusual and new. I considered what the limits on my ability to fight were. I looked at the clock on the wall of our sports hall, which was based in a former Lutheran church, and found that half an hour had passed swiftly.

It can't be! Fifteen rounds already? The gong rang. "We'll wrap it up lads," said the coach, "get off home."

So I initiated a new law: There is no limit. The phrase rang within me like a bell. There is no limit and that would be my sole rule. Well, there is a limit but it is important to know what it should be. If you are unaware, well that is something else. The day before I had fought only three rounds and been dog tired. Today I had fought for fifteen and withstood them, as if made of some unbreakable glass. Walking past the mirrored wall where we shadow boxed, I took a look at myself. I earned a couple of bruises, the guys were conscientious, but it's okay, not like yesterday, I thought.

I have never forgotten the law I learned then and conserve it like some secret magical power, recalling it in hard times. It transpired that this law was as universal for me as the law of gravity. If I needed to learn the half-year technical course in a single night from notes taken by a girl I knew, if I did not sleep for a couple of nights because I had no time, or whether I drank that second glass of liquor and did not go off the rails; this principle applied everywhere. The law opened larger possibilities for me and I enjoyed these to the best of my ability.

One interesting instance of this was when I developed a problem in my eye and it began twitching during a training session. The doctor confirmed it was a tic, "It's nothing," he said, "but you'll need hypnotism." He wrote out a prescription.

The old hypnotist I saw circled around me and tried various things, but nothing worked. The old man had a lot of experience, "Young fella," he said, with a strong Odesa accent, "you're not susceptible to hypnosis because your self-esteem is too high. Maybe you could be susceptible to self-hypnosis. Can you imagine something that you can't resist?" he added with a sly grin. "You have to submit to yourself and it's vital to eradicate your own weaknesses, otherwise you'll become neurotic." He explained what I needed to do.

That evening my aunt and uncle went to visit their children and I arranged a self-hypnosis session. I turned off the lights in the room, sat in a chair and began staring unblinkingly at the nickel kettle on the windowsill. It was lit by a faint ray from a streetlamp. The main challenge was not blinking, tears flowed down my cheeks, but I kept insistently reminding myself that there were no limits. I sat like that for six hours. When my relations returned I looked away from the kettle and came round with some effort. The tic had vanished and never returned. I realised that this method was not at all bad and I used it when I had to endure a lot of pain; it was, on occasion, vital. Novocaine was ineffective for me as an anaesthetic and other substances were not available under cost-free soviet health care, neither were dental treatments, the removal of appendix and so on.

To continue on the subject of appendicitis, an event which occurred much later in life shook my faith in the coherence of my knowledge of universal laws. It was 1978 and now I had swopped my love of boxing for mountaineering. The group I was with was traversing the Upper Svaneti, a mountainous valley on the Enguri River in Georgia, when one of our party, a doctor, had an attack of acute appendicitis. His temperature rose and his condition deteriorated swiftly; it was vital that some action be taken and he knew he would have to perform the operation on himself. "If I lose consciousness, you won't be carrying me alive from these mountains," he added.

We stopped in a small settlement, which consisted of three old residential towers, and borrowed a large wall mirror from the locals. The doctor had some surgical supplies and planned to use these to operate on himself while looking in the mirror, but one of us would have to sew him up.

"I want someone who won't faint for this job," he said, and looked steadily at me.

I looked at him and thought that we were made from the same mould, he also knew the law.

I do not want to get bogged down in details, but it all turned out for the best, eventually. When an event is clearly determined by the no limit rule you remember it.

When I swapped boxing for mountaineering, and then skiing, I found many occasions to use the applications of the law. Nowhere else do you get as fatigued as in the mountains when hauling yourself up and descending their slopes, particularly on the descent when still carrying the forty kilogram back-pack you had dragged to the summit. So, down I went as I repeated, *no limits, no limits.*

My late mother repeatedly berated me for doing everything, in her words, *Like a madman.* I think she had probably guessed about my personal law. Her job as a mathematician meant she specialised in understanding laws. Her opinion of the law is still relevant even now while I write this story and everyone is asleep; it is two o'clock in the morning and I will stay up until I have finished, keeping with the spirit of my law.

So, when we were in the mountains, our company consisted of three adherents of the no limit law, including me. I had told them about the idea and they loved it. Going further, going for more. Initially we just walked in the mountains, then quickened our pace, then we ran bearing a load. We spent the whole day like that. So, with our training goal in mind, we ran in the mountains of our native Crimea once a week, either on a Saturday or Sunday. Forty kilometres without a break while it was daylight.

We once decided to run from Krasnolissia to Yalta and unwittingly crossed a government reserve on our route. There was a large scale hunt going on, or maybe the officials were just resting! They had probably spotted us because we heard a helicopter on a nearby, treeless, hill. A whole division of marines was pouring out of its belly and were pursuing us. We had an advantage of about two hundred metres, and the distance to Yalta would not get any shorter. We could have run quicker than we did to get away, but were scared they would start shooting; so we ran steadily, dangling ourselves like carrots before our pursuers until they were utterly exhausted. Towards the end only one of our pursuers, a lieutenant, was left.

"Stop" he yelled, "I only want to talk."

We waited for him. He approached us and was almost totally out of breath; his tongue was lolling out of his mouth as he panted. "Well lads, you're as swift as horses, you've given us a right run around. You'd be all right in Afghanistan."

"You what," I replied, "we're peaceful people, though we have no limit."

He looked suspiciously at me and said, "Something here's off. Tell me more."

"No," I continued "that's it. You just need to know the locality."

We parted peacefully, but his suspicions remained. He told me this when I met up with him again in a very precarious situation. Maybe I'll write about it later, if I dare…

The special glory of these training sessions spread around the narrow circle and eventually a delegation from the Caucasus came to see us; two men and a woman. The older of the men spoke first, "We want to run with you through the mountains," and added, "and then tell the whole tale."

"What," we said surprised, "and the girl too?"

"I'm a professional guide," she said irritably, "we'll see you tomorrow."

The next morning we selected one of the very longest slopes, "We'll step up the pace all the time and if any of you fall behind, we'll wait for you up there on the high ground," we told them.

We set off slowly to begin with, and then quicker and quicker. Ten minutes later we were running as if it were a one hundred metre sprint. The older man had never expected us to reach such a pace. The woman was the first to fall behind, then one of the men, then another sat on the path, holding his side and gasping. We reached the top and lay down to sunbathe. It was about twenty minutes before the breathless rear-guard of this great army reached us. They obviously did not know the law. After this we received no more challenges and eventually we got bored of running in the mountains and gave up doing it.

I began to apply the law now and then and it never failed.

I had been a lanky child and other boys my age looked much sturdier. I had suffered emotionally because of my weediness, so I bought some dumb-bells and began to catch them up; I also did pull ups and push ups. So it went on. In time my life became restless. It is not possible to find a horizontal bar for pull ups everywhere, nor carry weights around, but you can do push ups everywhere. More than half a century has passed and I still do them, it is now a habit. Before I knew about the law I did forty push ups each time, after the law was revealed I did one hundred, and then the same again. Why one hundred? I like the number.

Years passed and I passed with them. A trivial phrase, but it reflected reality precisely. I continued to apply the law in daily life, but especially in situations when maximum effectiveness and efficiency were needed. This helped me to acquire new specialisations in education, business and in relations with those around me. When your partners suspect that you always have more to give, it clearly restricts their ability to manoeuvre against you. So, with time I developed a sincere affection for all tests and challenges. Where if not here, if not now, when?

Once I learned about the existence of an informal club of skiers and skateboarders who had the same name as my law;

No Limits. I immediately saw myself as a member.

Once, while skiing in Zermatt, Switzerland, I asked a local I knew where the hardest track was. He gave me directions to somewhere deep in the mountains. I journeyed for a long time, swapping from one cable car to the next until I came to a weird slope. It was very long, steep and, I thought, quite irregular. I ascended there finally on a little creaking aluminium wagon. I was alone inside it and checked out the many inscriptions and autographs scratched inside with sharp objects. One in particular interested me. Hem. Hemingway! Wow … it was dated from before World War Two. I checked out some others. Gina - surely Gina Lollobrigida. Finally, reaching the highest point of the descent, I ended up in the company of some unshaven Anglophones, some were on skis, some were on skates.

"Let's see who's fastest," one of them suggested.

"The last one gets in a round of whisky," threw in another.

There was a little bar at the bottom of the mountain, which I thought would serve as a place to have a jar.

The slope was bumpy and uneven, but I had seen similar at Cheget. I agreed, of course, and we had terrific races down the mountain, which were sometimes distracted by visits to the bar. After a couple of hours I was part of the gang and realised this was a meeting of the *No Limits* club. Fate occasionally brought me into contact with other members of the group, where those not in our fraternity would never ski.

After 1992 I noticed that the phrase *no limits* was being imbued with new significance in places like Russia and Ukraine. And few liked it. The words 'chaos' and 'guy with no limits' began to have a distinctly negative commutation. It was a shame because they were such important words for me. Without limits came to mean a violation of the unwritten rules (concepts) which received a sharp condemnation from both the business world and the underground. There was a conscious removal of moral and other limits in relations with partners and a reliance on force. The sole right that existed was the right of the strong to dominate society

I had occasion to meet with such predators, who were not the best representatives of the human race. The evolution of business dealt harshly with them. They have become extinct over time as a class and now I practically never encounter them. This pleases me, for the law continues to operate.

Thanks to the law I sat on a horse for the first time when I was over fifty, mastered the basics of the writer's craft when I was over sixty, having never studied equestrianism or writing before. Subsequently, I decided to study the history of my law. I found there were many adherents who followed the motto, *Nothing is too much,* which was the inscription on the shield of King Richard the First of England, or Richard Couer de Lion, Lionheart of the Plantagenet dynasty. He lived in the twelfth century and is remembered by history as a model of chivalry. And what are his words if not a paraphrase of the aphorism by Solon, an Athenian politician and legislator. For him too 'nothing is too much'. He formulated his principle twenty-seven centuries ago. And that is just what we know. So we can say my law and I are in good company.

After my sixtieth birthday I began to think about the limits of the applicability of my law. I had a sneaking suspicion that the limits exist somewhere. One day I would see them and ultimately feel them. It is possible that with time I will have to clarify the wording of the law for myself. It could read, *There are no limits, particularly for young, healthy, beautiful people.* But I really hope that day does not come soon.

And the ageing process? It would be interesting to apply the law to that. Perhaps our personal battle with age will last longer and we will tire less because of that. After all, Methuselah managed to clock up over nine hundred years … and when, after the flood, God limited our lifespan to one hundred and twenty years, it should be noted that people could not live for that long back then. The main thing is not age, but our attitude to it. The poet Yevgeny Yevtushenko wrote well on this theme:

There is
No yoke
Of years.
All of us falling foolishly in line with the herd
Invent age for ourselves.
But what kind of life is it
Limited by the self?
And not living.
Accost any old person,
Find the joker in them
And all these older women,
All these grey-haired girls
Their hair smooth as apple blossom
Till it withers and falls.

That's it. There's nothing else.

Don't Go Roaming in Africa, Kids

Parp, parp, parp … A harsh, intermittent sound pounded the air in the large room between decks; the sound was accompanied by a flashing red light. The crew began to stir and drag themselves from their beds. They moved in rows along the levels of the ship that was the height of a five-storey building. There was a whole battalion of privates and sergeants and I was the only officer on duty; stuck like everyone else on the eighth level.

I joined the army as a second year lieutenant in August 1968 and had taken part in a few Soviet Union army and navy operations. I had quite a pacific military speciality and was a signal man. For some reason, however, I was continuously seconded to the landing forces. This was probably due to my status as a bachelor and, to be honest, I was of an age when I liked travel and escapades, so this was just a new adventure to me. My squad was given a brigade of marines and we were sailing somewhere on a large landing ship. It was a military secret where, but according to rumour we were heading for Africa.

The tween-decks was being used as a temporary barracks and there was a duty officer stationed there. The battalion commander determined who it would be in the evening. "Lieutenant, it's your turn to be duty officer in the tween-decks," he told me.

"I've only just returned from being signal duty officer." I protested; I was enraged.

"So what," he replied, without turning a hair, "you'll have a whole twenty-four hours to rest there." He added, "There is absolutely nothing to do, just lie down until your stint is over. If I send someone more senior, they'll pull a blanket over his head and beat the crap out of him. You're not yet an enemy in their eyes and they're okay with you."

It was true. I had come from a civilian university, not

from school, so I did not fit in with the chain of command. I ran through the obstacle course alongside the privates and did my boxing training. I became friends with many of them and some are still my friends. As I have said before, I was the only officer in the boxing section of our unit.

For me there was no antagonism with the lower ranks and so I went on duty. But the signals, the red light and blaring noise, meant the end of our voyage had come. We needed to leave of our level of the ship fast, but I only managed to slowly climb up the narrow, metal ladders. When going down it was possible to slide down them swiftly by just holding the metal rail, providing you ensured your coat sleeve was between your hands and the rail or your hand would burn with the friction. The main thing was to run off quickly at the bottom or the next man would land on your head. Before the signal it was customary to lie fully dressed in a military greatcoat with an automatic to hand.

Our large, landing ship berthed, its hull opened on both sides and the ramp popped up. I checked the time; it was four in the morning. A barely visible mountainous coast, perhaps a stony beach, lay fifteen metres away across the dark waters. We knew the ship could not draw any closer as we all looked warily at the water. We were wearing overcoats and gun belts, and carried automatics; we would vanish without a trace in that water.

The commander and the other officers appeared and bellowed, "Forward Communists!"

No one moved with especial swiftness. The commander peered into the disordered rabble of soldiers and saw me, lacking sleep and unshaven, before he reformulated his order and bellowed, "Advance Lieutenant Finkelstein."

He got me. Even during the Czechoslovakian campaign I had been accepted as a candidate for membership of the Soviet Communist Party, who would take you in without delay if you

68

were at the front of the queue. The commander had picked me out very carefully, knowing I was in line to join and would not risk losing that chance.

The other soldiers were watching as I approached the edge of the ramp and plopped into the water. It reached my waist and was pretty cold. I screamed, "Follow me." The soldiers followed and soon we were all wet, angry and left on a deserted rocky beach. I noticed several other landing vessels berthing on the coast, with soldiers also jumping into the water. It was like the song about Nestor Makhno, *And the beach was covered with thousands hewed down and shot.* Of course, we were all alive and okay.

Suddenly, a shot came from somewhere above us on the rocky coast, then another, then a short burst of fire. Judging by the sound, it was a *Kalashnikov.* It seemed that the beach was not as abandoned as we had thought. Nevertheless, we ran and stormed the heights of the coast and eventually halted; having encountered no one. We were soaked through and water squelched in our boots; we were also very hungry.

Using my initiative I commandeered the troops, "Get dry, sort out your uniforms and eat."

We gathered driftwood and kindled a fire, got out our dry rations, and emptied the water from our boots. One hour later the sun rose and we felt rested and quite ready to fight. Twenty minutes later it was blazingly hot and we knew we were in Africa. Finally, the officer corps materialised. They were all clean shaven and fragrant with the coffee they had enjoyed over a leisurely breakfast. "Lieutenant Finkelstein," the commander said, having picked me out again, "why are you so dishevelled?"

My patience finally gave way, "Can I have a word in your ear Commander?"

"You can." The commander was slightly irritated by my request but clearly curious to know what it was.

I leaned towards him, for he was shorter. In a whisper,

but clearly enunciating the words, I told him in expletive-laden language just what I thought about all this. He looked at me in amazement but, I thought, even approvingly. "So, why are you sitting here, go back to the ship to shave and wash."

"But I'm on duty and haven't been relieved of my post," I replied. It was just like something out of an Arkady Gaidar tale.

These were little things, but the process had its own momentum. Those in charge were now here and peering through binoculars deep inland. A messenger approached and handed some missive to our commander, who gathered us together on the dune. "We've been ordered to carry out reconnaissance in force," he advised.

A unit of marines would be dispatched with a signal officer to operate a radio transmitter. I was the only signal officer so off I went. We packed ourselves tightly into two *UAZ* trucks and set off. One of the marines was also a lieutenant but not a two-year conscript from university like me; he was a career soldier who had worked his way up the ranks and was unknown to me.

Our all-terrain vehicles crawled laboriously over the trackless ground. After two hours we saw some pitiable shacks which comprised a village. They were empty except for one, inside which a local woman of uncertain age sat. She did not react to us and seemed to be ill. We went further until one of our vehicles broke down. "The engine has stuck, it has been in storage for too long," the driver informed us sombrely.

The situation heated up literally and figuratively. Heat ripples were mirage-like over the sun-scorched African earth. I tried to call base but got no reply, there was just static crackling on the radio and the signal was weak; this was twenty years before the mobile phone era began.

We unpacked a tent from the other vehicle to make space and crammed into the truck like a bunch of grapes.

70

We travelled slowly, knowing it would be very bad if this one stalled too. Three hours later we reached the coast and found no landing ships berthed there. We had missed the area.

The other lieutenant fell ill at this point and lost consciousness, his pulse was weak and irregular; it looked like sunstroke. There were eleven of us, one of whom was now quite sick. I was the only officer and needed to make a decision. We improvised a shack from the tent in the vehicle. I injected the sick man with an anecdote and gave him the remaining, albeit warm, fresh water from his canteen. I estimated that the landing area was to our right and hoped I was not mistaken. I planted the driver and three soldiers in the truck and ordered them to head there directly along the coast, but not to travel further than thirty kilometres, and if they found nothing to head back to us.

It was four in the afternoon according to my watch and soon the drug began to work and the lieutenant regained consciousness, but could not get to his feet. Three hours passed before we finally heard a helicopter. I was a little worried and wondered whose aircraft it could be. It transpired that it had taken off from the deck of one of our landing ships.

We arrived back at the base and were given a telling off by the top brass. But that meant nothing to us by the time evening drew in, we were all sick with a temperature of forty degrees and had red sores on our skin. The village, I thought, no wonder it was empty.

We were taken somewhere before being dispatched from a field airbase on a medical aircraft to Sevastopol and then moved very cautiously to a hospital. As an officer I was allocated to the general's ward for the higher ranks. The soldiers were all dispatched to an ordinary ward. I later found out that the other lieutenant had only needed treating for sunstroke. The infectious disease had passed him by.

I was kept in isolation on the ward and my food was

slipped under the door on something that resembled a large wooden spatula. A doctor in a white decontamination suit entered and injected me with what I was told was an experimental drug. My optimism faded at this point, but a few days passed and I began to recover very quickly.

"It's a pity you were ill for such a short time. I could have written a thesis about you," the doctor said.

"What was my illness?"

"Only the devil knows," he replied, and went on to tell me that they had simply recorded in my case notes that I had suffered from some unknown tropical disease. I live with its legacy to this day.

I began to notice that the nurses who came to my room had changed. Previously they had been older women, now they were young and shapely. The doctor enlightened me when he told me that a young officer, who was laid up but recovering quickly and still unmarried, would lure them in. Some others married, say an army political officer, while still at school, but that was a rarity here. Nurses brought potential brides to look over a fiancé, and these would-be brides were their daughters, nieces and other relatives. I realised that much longer here and I would be married and discharged early back home to Simferopol.

They were waiting for me for a roll call where I served as an officer. It was called a roll call rather than what it was, an examination. I do not know why, even now. I began grumbling when I got there, "Let me rest, I can't come back and serve yet because of my health."

"You can rest when you're a pensioner," the battalion commander snarled. However, he looked me over and dispatched me to roam in the fresh air, or in other words he gave me two days to patrol the city. They assigned two young soldiers to me so we could help maintain order.

That evening in the city park, which would later be

called the *Zelenka*, we roamed idly. There were many people around and I saw a group of military conscripts from the ranks of those who were used to escort prison convoys. They were drinking vodka next to the park fence and swearing raucously. I approached and warned them. Yes, I was a respectable military veteran in uniform with a gun at my side, I thought.

I caught a movement out of the corner of my eye and swayed sharply to the side, so the punch only partially connected. My cap fell and just like in a training session I turn and delivered a straight right smack to the middle of that drunken face. Something crunched under my fist and I realised I had broken his nose. My own nose had been smashed twice previously so I knew how unpleasant it was. My own soldiers had scarpered somewhere and I found myself under a hail of blows. I reached for my gun but something heavy hit my hand. The gun fell and I pulled it back by the strap attached to the ring of its butt, grabbed it and fired into the air. My attackers ran and I was left alone in an empty space.

I saw my timid soldiers hiding under a bush. No one could hold me back. I rushed to the command post and raised the alarm before I went around all the military chambers. By morning the perpetrators were sitting in cells at the Simferopol headquarters, but not all of them; the one who had hit me and received a blow in exchange was placed under guard in a military hospital. I wrote a report and with a sense of achievement went home to bed. When I looked in the mirror at home, I saw I had a shiner under my eye.

At noon the following day I powdered the bruise and went to headquarters for another stint on duty. I was summoned by the commandant of the city. My report lay on his desk. "Resisting a patrol is a serious crime," he said, "but you can rewrite the report if you like."

"Why would I do that?" I said, "it's all true."

"It will mean five years in a disciplinary battalion for

them, but I don't insist on you changing it, go and have a think."

I walked out of his door and found myself among a crowd of the soldiers' agitated relatives. The men were local, Crimean, and their parents had come when the news of their plight had been raised. Their fathers tried to ply me with drink; their mothers tried to soften me up, and their sisters ogled the young officer who had jailed their brothers. I was not made of iron and two hours later I broke and rewrote the report. The soldiers, now guilty only of drunkenness rather than resisting orders, sat in the guardhouse for two weeks before returning to service. I forgot about it a week later when I was occupied with other matters.

Interestingly, the man who had instigated the fight was from Simferopol. Many years later I would bump into him almost every day in the street as we went to work. We struck up an acquaintance and I learned that since our encounter he had been to university, graduated and become a teacher, then a head teacher. Every time we met he stretched out his hand, looked into my eyes and said, "Good health to you Comrade Lieutenant."

I lost track of him over time, but I am pleased I rewrote that report. Who knows what can happen in life? There are not enough jails for everyone. Yesenin, who was steeped in Russian life and customs, on the back of his own experience wrote on this theme:

Which of us on the deck of the large ship
Has not fallen, vomited and cursed?
There are only a few experienced souls
Who remain strong as the ship rolls?

And what about marriage? I just had three months left to roam free as it transpired. Was it worth resisting?

In the Desert

The clock on the wall indicated it was already two in the afternoon and time for dinner. I was twenty-three, in the army and on duty for our section. It was tedious but it did have its advantages, one of which was that I got to sample lunch in the canteen and assess its quality. Because I was in the upper echelons I suspected that it was not always an accurate assessment and they selected a bigger portion, albeit from the same pot as the soldiers. The food was pretty satisfying, even if it was monotonous, but I did notice that the soldiers put on weight.

I was still eating when a messenger approached me with a missive summoning me to the headquarters. When I arrived, the captain, deputy of the chief of staff, advised me that I was being dispatched to undertake further education.

"What kind of education," I grumbled, "isn't my university degree enough? Half the officers don't have higher education." I should add that the journeys, missions, and study involved in military life had left me feeling pretty bored with it all. Not once had I managed to worm out of doing these jobs since the very beginning of my service. I was really feeling the privation of my bachelor existence with all this.

"You're being dispatched to a course in desert combat. Collect your instructions, travel information and tickets, and sign here; you're leaving for Ashkhabad tomorrow."

That seemed far away to me and I knew it would probably be very hot because it was already May.

"Will it take long?"

"It'll be as long as it'll take, but if you believe the paper, a month and a half." His answer baffled me, but there was nothing to do but get on with it.

I arrived in Turkmenistan on the evening of the following day. Thirty officers had also flown in from different parts of our then motherland. They gathered us into local army headquarters, and planted us on buses. We journeyed by road for five hours and arrived at a lonely military settlement. All around us stretched the Karakum desert.

Training began the following day and, as you might expect, consisted of theory and practice. We studied military materiel, vehicles, weapons and communication equipment, as well as methods of warfare. Particular attention was paid to physical and psychological training, hand to hand combat, shooting with every kind of armament, and surviving extreme conditions. I was surprised by some of the topics. It seemed as if we were preparing for combat operations or working as small subversion groups, isolated from the main armed forces. There were exercises to develop independence and initiative, qualities not always encouraged in the lumbering, rusty mechanism of the army of the Soviet Union. They usually liked soldiers to accurately execute their orders and no more.

"Never trust anyone when in combat," an old lieutenant colonel with a large scar on his forehead urged us, "only trust yourself and then not always."

"Who should we trust then?" we piped up.

"Your inner voice, your intuition," he replied calmly. "The intuition of a participant in military action is always more accurate because it is built on correct, unbiased information."

A major, who was also a psychologist, explained to us that the world was as we perceived it to be; if we perceived it in an agitated state that would negatively affect our world; we should therefore remain optimistic and calm, even in the most helpless situation. This clearly ran counter to the materialist conceptions of Marxist-Leninist philosophy, but it sounded convincing.

We practiced shooting both soviet and non-soviet weapons, but the course involving off-road driving was of particular interest to me because it provided me with a welcome change from regular military activities.

The survival classes were taught by a colourful, bearded, civilian specialist and were also absorbing; I need to go into detail about the hand to hand combat training in order to complete my story. The classes were led by a thirty-five year old captain, who looked like a martial arts specialist. He was my height, with an athletic build and a shaved head. Vague rumours that he was suspected of sodomy circulated, but there was no direct evidence so perhaps it was just the idle chatter of the local servicemen on the evening of our arrival. I attempted a not very successful joke along the lines of, *I don't approve, but everyone's entitled to do what they like with their own ass.* Subsequent events were evidence that one of my drinking companions had relayed this information to the captain.

I was not familiar with the techniques of eastern martial arts, which formed the corps of his classes, but I had always been competitive, particularly in sports, and had already been a candidate for a higher degree in sports. But I had never seen anything like this. I did not like our relationship with the teacher. He bore himself in a very dry and formal manner, and addressed me only by my surname. When demonstrating exotic techniques in training he took the chance to be physically rough, even cruel, a couple of times. He never looked into my eyes then, although I knew he was not obliged to like me.

Under his training system he broke us up into pairs and chose a victim to humiliate as much as he could while supposedly demonstrating the technique. My turn to be abused came. Standing alongside him I did not look formidable and was not a martial arts specialist.

"Attack me," he commanded, and I reluctantly attempted a left jab.

Vasyl Ivanovich, for that was his name, seized my hand and without releasing it descended and rolled backwards over his head; simultaneously he thrust his feet into my chest,

I flew over him and my shoulder blades smacked harshly on the ground. A little dazed, I saw, as through a fog, a huge fist descending towards my face. An acute sense of danger and pain drew a lightning reaction from me, I rolled to the right and his fist knocked quite a hole in the densely packed earth where my head had been only a second ago. The bastard, I thought. Then I rolled in the opposite direction because he was leaping, with both legs together, on to my chest; luckily I had moved. Jumping to my feet, I tried to catch the look in his eyes; I needed no further evidence that he hated me.

I barely conquered my rage while the trainer had seemingly calmed down. During the remaining training sessions I was as prepared as I possibly could be and they passed by without any more alarming incidents. Like the rest of my group, I studied incessantly until the exams were due. I passed them all easily until only two remained, martial arts and survival.

The martial arts test required a candidate to undertake five minutes of freestyle sparring with the trainer. I suspected it would end badly for me, but, thankfully, by that age I had gained a lot of experience in both street fighting and the boxing ring. I learned that physical force and even sports techniques were far from all that a good fighter needed. When street fighting, the approach you use in the ring, mindful action and correct tactics, is important; in the past I had won sparring matches against strong favourites. I had always 'done my homework', going ahead of schedule to check out my opponents and thinking through every fight beforehand. I had reached the conclusion that my head had not been given to me so it could be soundly beaten by my supposed friends and comrades; I had received the honorary soubriquet 'The Crafty Boxer' while I was still in Odesa.

Now I sat and thought through the sparring session and did a little physical preparation. The examination was held over a three-day period, with ten candidates being tested by our uncongenial trainer each day. We were called in alphabetical order, which meant I was the last to have to face him on the day in question. At this point the students previously tested by him had acquired a sufficiency of injuries: A broken arm, a pair of broken ribs, broken noses, and an incalculable quantity of bruises was the tally so far. Something told me that he had saved his best and sweetest treats for me.

My turn finally came. I was wearing my boots and field uniform, including military jacket, but without the belt. We met in the middle of the sparring area. The test commission of two officers was sitting at a table to the side. My instructor pushed his face up to mine, "I'll bury you," he said quietly, with a polite smile, then tried to head-butt me in the face. I barely had time to jump, but managed to dance around him. He stood, unmoving, only turning his face to keep me in view. He's waiting for me to throw a hand in his direction, I thought and feinted with my left. His eyes flashed with delight and he stepped forward to catch my sleeve, but I kicked him in the knee with the toe-end of my boot. He fell, clutching his leg, and I ran over to him, raising my fist.

"Punch his lights out," yelled one of the spectators who had suffered from his attentions earlier. But I could not let myself do that; punching someone on the floor, and indeed kicking someone in the knee, is beyond the laws of boxing.

I turned and approached the invigilators' table. The head of the commission was an elderly colonel. His eyes widened suddenly and I soon realised what was happening and spun while crouching. A terrifying kick whistled above me. That would have got my head, you twat, I thought and jumped forward while spinning to deliver a blow with my right hand. Take this you fucker, you should've finished me off. The blow did not land properly and I hurt my knuckles, but this new mentor was felled like the last one.

The five minutes was over and I had passed, but there

was still the survival exam waiting for me. It was not long before I was advised of the conditions for the test.

"You'll be dropped off from a helicopter into the desert with a flask of water and a radio transmitter. No food. You'll have to survive for three days. Do that and you've passed. In an emergency, contact the base. You'll be in field uniform without your greatcoat. The soul luxury you'll have is a green uniform and a hat with a brim instead of the usual cap. You'll have a knife, matches and a gun … but no bullets."

I consider this thoroughly and stuck eight bullets for my pistol in the lining of my boots. That'll come in handy, I thought, what use is a pistol without bullets? Am I supposed to strike sparks with it?

I was deposited on a sand dune in the desert at five o'clock in the morning. The helicopter took off and I got to work. The sun had not long risen; it was still not too hot, but I knew that in two or three hours it would be thirty-five degrees Celsius and it would be quite cold at night. I had read about the area in some guidance notes; they advised me that it had a sharply continental climate. I dug myself into the sand up to my neck so only my eyes showed, and covered the top of my head with my hat, which was slightly moistened with water from my flask. I hoped that the water would reduce the temperature around the top of my head as it evaporated. So I sat, or rather stood, like that until sunset. Something moved in the sand, crawling and biting, but it was endurable and I managed to tolerate being unable to meet my body's natural needs.

The sun had no sooner dipped over the horizon when the temperature dropped perceptibly. I extracted myself from the sand and loaded my revolver; then I gathered some branches, kindled a small fire and searched for something to eat. I anticipated shooting some animals but there was nothing until I noticed a green lizard wriggling across the sand. Approaching the animal stealthily I grabbed its tail, which broke off and was left wriggling in my hand. The lizard scarpered, but I had the tail at least. I skinned it with my knife and, piercing it with a twig for a spit, roasted the tail over the fire. I ate it warily, but it was quite palatable.

The temperature after sunset was extremely cold, so I dug myself in again. The sand had kept me cool earlier, but also retained the daytime heat so I knew it would keep me warm at night. Unfortunately, the living things in the sand were more active at night, but I could do nothing about it. The night passed, then a day.

During the next night, at about two in the morning, I heard a helicopter and emerged from my sandy refuge. The new moon illuminated the very dark night and I could see the helicopter had landed a couple of dunes away from my position. Two men disembarked from it, but something quelled any urge I had to call out to them, Don't trust anyone, I thought, and crept stealthily closer to them.

"Where will you put him?" I heard someone ask.

"Yes, Kolenka, I'll bury him somewhere here, no one'll find him," came the reply.

There were two officers, both armed, one of whom was Vasyl Ivanovich; I did not know the other. A carousel of thoughts swirled around my head. I had one clip of ammunition; eight bullets. When lying down with a support for a gun I did not miss a target, however, I had only shot targets and really did not want to shoot real people. Besides, I could not shoot too straight with only a pistol and I could not bury a helicopter. I knew shooting them was not an option.

I crawled back and again hid myself in the sand. My foe walked around the area and called out to me for fifteen minutes before boarding the helicopter and taking off. A sudden impulse got into me, I emerge from the sand and crept closer. While the engine roared and its blades churned sand and air I took aim with my Makarov pistol and shot off the tail light. They would not hear it but when they got back they would know I could have killed them.

Another day passed and a helicopter arrived in the evening. It was the same aircraft, less its tail light. Two men emerged from it, one of whom was the chair of the commission.

"Is that all?" I asked.

"You're alive then?" the colonel said in astonishment as he appeared. I thought he looked worried. "Your radio wasn't responding and you didn't call anyone."

"Well, like you said, we needed to last three days."

"What the hell are you up to with your three days? We said that to test your courage, one day would have been enough, we picked up the others yesterday; two have sunstroke and are in the sickbay. You seem quite perky I see."

"Aha," I said as I boarded the helicopter first and saw the pilot. It was the one who had accompanied the captain. "What's happened to your tail lights?" I enquired, leaning towards him and yelling so that he could hear through the headset, "I might have shot you in the head but for the lack of anything to bury the helicopter with." Unable to restrain myself I added, "And tell Vasyl to watch his ass."

We returned to the base and I spent the night with the other trainees, prudently avoiding being at risk. We were given the results the following day and sent home.

"Lieutenant Finkelstein, tell us honestly how you managed to spend three days in the desert without even getting tanned?" the colonel and commission chair asked before I left.

"It's a particular attribute of my body."

"You're lying," said the colonel confidently, "but who knows given your historic motherland and your ancestors' forty years of wandering in the wilderness. Perhaps that is your place."

So, I became an unresolved enigma in the chronicles of courses on desert combat. However, fate would bring me up against Vasyl Ivanovich again, but I will tell you about that later.

Inspection

The rain had poured down overnight, there were puddles everywhere and everything was sodden, but the sun was already rising. It was a mild autumn day in November 1969. I had risen early, washed, shaved, eaten breakfast and was now dressed and wearing my ammunition, ready for inspection. It was an established tradition that inspections would occur regularly and my division was due one.

I was prepared well in advance and had put on my drill uniform yellow-gold belt. My wife had sewn gold epaulettes to my great coat. As an officer, who had joined from university, I did not need a separate greatcoat for parade-ground drill and only needed to change the epaulettes on the one I had. I donned my parade-ground cap and my polished boots and was ready.

"You're ahead of schedule," my wife said, "pop to the shop for some bread."

I darted out of the door unhesitatingly, after all the shop was only in the next residential block. Everyone in the shop looked at me approvingly, I knew what they were thinking: *So young and already a proper lieutenant.* Indeed, I was only twenty-three and had graduated from university, served successfully in the army and started a family seven and a half months ago. It seemed to me that I had completed the mandatory programme required by life and was quite pleased with myself. It transpired this was all only the beginning, but what did I know about life then.

After buying a loaf, I strode briskly to the exit and crossed the threshold. It was muddy outside so a metal mesh in a wooden frame lay before the doors for customers to wipe their feet before going in. It was out of respect for the work of the cleaners. Their labours were praised in the flowery language the soviets used for workers on a poster attached to a nearby wall. I trod on the mesh as I exited the shop but it unexpectedly skated from under my feet and I sprawled forward, right into a puddle. Water splashed merrily into the air and my cap flew off my head, rolled and lay in a neighbouring puddle. The only thing unscathed was the loaf because I had the foresight to raise my arm as I fell. I had plunged face-first into the mud and must have looked quite a sight. I jumped up and looked around; passers-by were in awe of the spectacle I presented. I hurried home, smeared from top to toe in mud.

"What on earth happened to you?" chirped my young wife and visiting mother-in-law when I returned.

"I fell in a puddle and need to get it sorted quickly, I'm now running late."

The two women grabbed rags, brushes and a bucket of water, and swiftly washed away all traces of my tumble, but now I was soaked. I would dry off on the journey so was not too worried about it. I quickly headed to my post. I did not have a car back then and went to my destination through a short cut across an old cemetery, which was far quicker than going the long way around on a trolleybus. I reached the military settlement and wriggled through a gap into the fence and into the parade ground where everyone was already in place. The battalion commander looked at me miserably, but did not say anything, and I plunged into my spot.

The drill began. We marched to the low rostrum on which the divisional commander stood, he was accompanied by a commission headed by an elderly, as I thought then, general from the military district.

"Halt in line," commanded the officer on our right flank. We saw the head of the commission approaching. The sun was hotter now and he was without a greatcoat, but wore uniform belts crossed and boots with solid, shiny leggings; a dapper general indeed. We were roasting in our overcoats; the order for swapping to winter uniforms had been signed the previous week.

"Good morning Comrade Lieutenants," he said as he walked along the line of officers.

"Good health to you Comrade General."

"I congratulate you on the commencement of this inspection."

"Hurrah!" we all roared amicably in unison.

"Do you have any points to make, or suggestions?"

We all kept quiet. The fact was that we were being paraded in ranks just so we did not embarrass our commanders. Everyone understood that it was not a good idea to wash your dirty linen in public. The army as a whole condemned it. So no one ever raised an issue. Then the general turned his attention to me. I had not managed to dry off.

"Why are you wet? Have you pissed yourself?" he asked acerbically.

"No sir," I replied dourly, "I fell into a puddle."

"A soviet lieutenant should not fall into a puddle and should wring out his uniform sharpish."

"I did wring it out," I replied, but the general had moved on and was not listening.

He was thin, smartly turned out, with a bushy grey moustache, and looked about fifty. He walked lightly, as if dancing, and clearly enjoyed the whole process of the inspection. Then he stopped, looked at our brightly polished, but rumpled, boots and said, as if confidingly, "The lieutenant's boots are rumpled like an accordion, but his penis is cylindrical, it's the other way round for a general, yes?"

We cackled happily and, pleased with the result of his joke, he walked to a nearby group of officers. The inspection lasted for four hours. By the end my clothes had dried on the outside, but were soaked with sweat on the inside. It was completely dark by the time we had finished, so I clambered through the hole in the fence I had used earlier and headed homewards in a happy mood. Everyone passed to and fro through the hole, officers and men alike, but no one spoke of its secret aloud or dared to seal it up. It had existed for a while but I had only checked it recently.

The road homewards lay, as I have said, across a large, old, redundant cemetery. The well-trodden path meandered between higgledy-piggledy stone crosses, there were no streetlights and the sliver of the crescent moon barely illuminated my way. I had penetrated far into the murk when there was a sudden scratching sound. One of the old crosses seemed to be swaying. Suddenly, a green face pushed out from it and said quietly, "Lieutenant, do you hear me? Lieutenant spare us some change for a drink?"

An apparition, I thought, maybe it's not talking to me. "What do they call you? I asked.

"Mishka."

"Are you alive?"

"Not yet, I need a drink."

I put my hand into my pocket and, groping around, found some small change and poured it into the outstretched palm before I cheerfully galloped off and was back home quickly. I had a cup of tea and went to bed. Tomorrow I would face new challenges as I undertook my duties.

From then on Mishka kept crossing my path. I never saw him in daytime, but only from late evening onwards. He no longer asked for money, instead he cadged cigarettes. Occasionally I brought him sandwiches from work. We did not speak much and always said one and the same thing.

"I wish you good health Lieutenant, how are things with you?"

"Everything's okay, Mishka."

"Well, bye then."

The cemetery seemed to be full of life at that time; noises, jostling shadows and distant cries, but Mishka seemingly enjoyed a certain authority here. No one else spoke to me. The place looked totally different at night, but when we met I noted the surroundings.

I passed through the cemetery in the morning as I went to work and wanted to know just where he came out of the ground and see it in daylight. I turned off the path and made my way to the moss-covered limestone cross. There was nothing remarkable nearby. I pushed the cross and with unexpected ease it swung on one of the metal pins connecting it to the large plate covering the tomb. The other pins seem to have been severed across the middle, but their outer parts remained. A rectangular opening, large enough for an adult male to pass through, was revealed in the centre of the tomb. I looked down into it, there was a small crypt below the cross which was empty except for an old, saggy mattress. What a hidey hole, I thought as I pushed the cross back into place and went on my way, life in a grave. The demon was in fact a tramp.

In the evening Mishka addressed me with a more substantive sentence. "Lieutenant, have you seen my house?"

"I've seen it, but it's an exaggeration to call it a house."

"Great, but I beg you not to tell anyone about it. It's very important to me."

"Okay," I agreed, and the topic was exhausted.

These encounters continued for a while until a couple of months later when I was going home by my usual route and there was a sudden noise, whistles and lights. I found a whole bunch of policemen surrounding me in the cemetery. When they saw me they were pretty puzzled.

"What are you doing here, Lieutenant?" the senior officer, a forty year old police major, asked sternly.

"I'm just going home."

"You'll have to come with us," he announced.

"Uh-oh, you're not my boss, we have our own commander here."

"Lieutenant, we can call the commander's office, but I assure you no good will come of it, it's better if we just have a talk and, if you are innocent, just take our leave of each other amicably."

I looked at his credentials; something inside told me it was not worth arguing. We drove to the police station where he told me that they had been investigating, and finally established, the route of some plant-based narcotics traffic from Central Asia to Crimea. It transpired that this 'Great Silk Road' ran across the old cemetery.

"Tell me, Lieutenant," he said, "didn't you notice anything suspicious?"

"No, there is sometimes a local tramp called Mishka who cadges cigarettes. A lot of obscure types hang out there, but they never come close."

"Mishka," sighed the major, "is the local boss, you could say he is a drugs lord. He's a Roma whom we've trailed for a long time, but can't get him. He's a ghost. And we didn't catch him today. Well, okay, off home with you."

I was two hours late returning home. Everyone was asleep, so I had a cold sausage sandwich for dinner. As I lay in bed I wondered where Mishka was, but guessed he must have many hideouts. The morning after I walked down the same path and found the spot. I crept through the bushes, gripped the cross and tried to move it. It did not budge an inch. I could not understand, it shifted before. The cross had stood cemented for all eternity into its stone plinth and from the outside looked as if it had stayed thus for fifty years. That was more or less the period according to the date chiselled in the stone slab.

I went on my way and a few days later I had almost completely forgotten the whole affair. I had many other things on my plate.

Six years later, in 1975, my army days were long behind me and I was working at the design institute where I headed a group of staff. During a business trip to central Asia I found myself in Bukhara. My job there was to collate research for developing a project concerning the tele-mechanisation of the local gas company, Bukharatransgaz. The friendly local comrades were showing us around the area and one day we visited a tea house where the food was generally much tastier than back home. Have a pilaf and you would be licking your fingers with relish, but everything seemed closed-in here. There were high fences and walls and everyone kept each to their own behind them. The ladies were attractive, they had black braids and wore round caps and satin dresses patterned in black and white. There were ancient ruins, long-collapsed libraries and observatories, so much, too much, that was fascinating.

The teahouse we visited was very popular and so it was essential to book a table or you would not get in. We were served a dish of pilaf and washed our hands. Our local colleagues showed us how to eat it with our fingers because mutton fat would trickle down your sleeve if you got it wrong. It is important to scoop up the fistful of rice with your fingers and carry it to your mouth, making sure your elbow is above your palm. I got the hang of it quickly and tucked in.

We were sitting on pillows on low benches, with a similarly low but wide table before us. A larger and jollier group was sitting to the side of us at another table. A burly, black-haired and black-eyed middle aged man sat at the head of it. They all spoke Uzbek, but it was clear everyone held him in high esteem. He was passed a large sheep's head and began carving into it with gusto.

We ate, drank some green tea, stood up, sat back down and ate and drank some more. The meal lasted three hours in total. I looked at the next table, the man eating the sheep's head was chewing the last pieces with difficulty. I would have burst if I had eaten that much and thought it would be enough for my entire group.

The sheep-head devourer rose and made his way towards the exit through the tables. Two young men from his party followed him closely. When they passed our table he stopped, stared at me and looked into my eyes. In a very clear voice he said, "Good morning Lieutenant, how are you?" Without waiting for an answer he continued, "Thank you for not spilling the beans. Have a good life."

"Mishka, is it you?" I asked, but he had moved on.

The locals stared at me in superstitious fear. "Do you know each other?" one of them asked.

"Yes, we've met," I replied, noticing how they all shivered in unison.

"Who is that man?" I asked my nearest neighbour quietly.

They did not reply and moved away from me a little for some reason. From that moment on and until my departure I was held in strange regard by all around. For some reason they began calling me sir, but they never asked to see me socially again.

When we left the tea house the waiter approached me and silently proffered a heavy paper bag. I looked inside and found it contained a bottle of Kabardino-Balkaskyi cognac, two packs of imported cigarettes and a piece of paper which simply said, *Thank you and Goodbye.* No signature; Mishka had repaid his debt.

Three days later I returned home. The first thing I did was visit the old cemetery and found the place where I had first met Mishka. I gripped the cross and pulled. It stood fast. I turned to leave and then I saw a piece of paper. It must have been crushed against the stone plinth somehow. The wind blew it up from the pedestal and flipped it over. The words, *I said goodbye,* were written on it.

The cemetery was demolished a couple of years later and is now the site of a military school. A bank stands on the site of the shop where this story began. I walked past it yesterday.

From A to B

To pass between A and B as quickly as possible by traversing the shortest distance *AND* staying alive ... that can be said to be the essence of all mountain sports, mountain tourism, proper mountain hiking, mountaineering, climbing and skiing. So, consider why this should not form a philosophy for your life; in my opinion quite a fitting one. In reality, however, everything occasionally does not meet that model in part, or indeed in full. The winners in life are not often those who travel the straight paths - and where do you find those anyway? And who do you go with, someone in the team or someone who is for or against them?

Thirty years ago I was a member of a group of mountain climbers traversing a training route along the passes of the Main Caucasian Ridge. There were five of us, our mission was intended to last four or five days and we were already on the return leg of our route. We had forty kilometres of snow-covered mountain left to traverse; a journey of two days in theory. We moved slowly as we carried our packs, tired from our three-day passage over the mountains. Who drove us to risk our heads in this adventure? No one but me; my energy had no other outlet and I wanted to test my capability.

We moved across several parallel gorges, traversing long distances up and down the mountain sides so many times. It was worse going down than up, as everyone who has experience of mountaineering knows. While we traversed the next gorge, one of our party saw that the entire opposite slope was moving. I saw a massive wall of snow hurtling towards us as he cried, "Avalanche." We broke into a run, heading upwards with our heavy backpacks because we did not have time to cast them aside. At the top of the gorge we wordlessly darted into a pocket in the rock of the next gorge along. Its rear wall shielded us from the avalanche. We bunched together as the snow cascaded, rumbling over our heads and hurling itself over the mountain crest. In a few seconds it had sealed our refuge, transforming it into a cramped and utterly dark dungeon. We waited a few minutes before we got our spades and began carefully digging our way out. It was good snow and not too tightly packed, so the lower layers moved easily.

After an hour and a half we had dug a narrow tunnel through the seven-metre thick mass of snow and were able to climb out. What we saw astounded all of us. The landscape had changed radically; everything was immersed in a thick layer of snow. The gorge was no longer so deep, but the most alarming thing was that not all the snow had come down with the avalanche; huge static waves of it hung ready to descend. We could see another avalanche would happen at any second. We decided to abandon our backpacks, carry small, emergency rations in our pockets, strap on our skis and try to reach our base camp during daylight. We had a chance because dawn had not long broken.

We set off carefully at first and then raced down slopes or stepped sideways up them. We were completely exhausted after six hours and it was clear we had little chance of surviving the nocturnal cold. Then we broke the cardinal rule of survival in the wilderness, we ate the emergency rations. During the last ascent to our base, which was on a mountain slope, we threw off our skis, but night came in very swiftly.

The toughest aspect of this situation was not the race or the maximum expenditure of physical and spiritual strength, it was our need to account for the state-owned property buried somewhere in the mountains. We were hassled constantly and were compelled to write numerous reports; the powers that be even tried to prosecute us and only calmed down when we committed ourselves to cover the costs from our meagre engineers' salaries. Even though I was a team leader in the design institute and worked twelve-hour days I only received a wretched one-hundred and seventy roubles each month. We were expected to pay back the money from our pathetically low salaries before the next mountaineering season, while also feeding our families. One of our party noted that it was fortunate a helicopter had not been sent for us or we would have needed to pay for our lives.

This financial set-back did not dampen our ardour. One year later we were back in the mountains. It was only possible to drink so much vodka and watch so many tedious socialist realist films while lying on the sofa. That life had no interest for any of us. We only spoke about being in the mountains when we met. Normal people who were part of those chats thought we were a bit strange.

When I read one of my official evaluations for working abroad, twenty years after it had been originally drafted, I came across a striking phrase under the drawbacks section. I was criticised as being 'inclined to organise informal groups of people to engage in winter sports'. Well, whoever had written that was right, I was 'inclined'. It was another thing whether *they* would not have jailed me with an evaluation of that kind in those days. The document was handed to me with my membership card and the remnants of my personal file after the termination of the soviet communist party. Despite this evaluation I was permitted to work abroad; with an evaluation like that I could have ended up assigned to some hell hole where I could have caught malaria or yellow fever.

But let us take a broader view; there are many A and B points in life, we all know point A, where we set off from, and, happily, are ignorant of point B, where we end up, however, there are a great many different points in between. Every goal is from A to B, so is every path we take and every encounter.

The road is life, I say not for the first time, and it is what I really think, but some do not make this journey within life. They sit and play around and believe that they are impelled towards point B, but their mistake is that if they do not move towards that last point B, it approaches them sure enough - and occasionally far quicker than it should.

One year after the avalanche, we were dreaming about the next mountaineering season in January 1980. We had bought the tickets to travel in December 1979, assembled the group in our homes and worked out the plan for our trip. We were regularly dreaming about our future adventures, however, my plans were brought to an abrupt halt when I received an urgent telegram from the ministry requiring me to appear at a collegial meeting regarding the deaths of two people due to an industrial accident.

I was puzzled by this request, but I soon found out it was because I had designed the engineering works on a building in which there was a production facility and a built-in garage. It had been constructed and was operating fine and dandy until one, not such a great, day when a driver had invited a woman on a date in the garage. We all know 'there was no sex in the Soviet Union' but what they got up to could be given a different name. It was cold in the garage so he had started up the engine to keep them warm. Alas, they both died from the exhaust fumes because they did not turn off the engine or make sure the place was ventilated.

I knew about this business but did not think it concerned me; it was a private tragedy. Oh, it concerned me right enough! The accident had occurred during working time and someone had to be punished for the deaths of two builders of communism. They summoned the director and the chief project engineer, me. "Someone will get banged up for this," muttered armchair experts in smoking rooms at the plant.

The director slowly picked up the report and made a decision. Ten minutes later they had arranged for me to take a trip to see those in charge at government level, and the very next day I was at the ministry. My affair was the last item on the agenda of the board and I had to wait outside the door for two hours. They called me in eventually and the minister, who was very formidable, asked who I was.

"The chief project engineer," I replied.

"Where's the director?"

"He's ill."

"So, he's really not coming?"

In reply I blurted out the wrong thing because the tension had clearly affected me. Instead of answering modestly with the words, I do not know, I mumbled more than enough in my confusion, "I don't watch over my director."

Our minister was a famous rural wit, but now he looked at me with undisguised curiosity and asked, "So, you are standing in for him?"

I was finally dumbstruck at this point and just nodded my head.

"Well, let's begin," he thundered overpoweringly.

After the report from the department of health and safety at work, I realised what I was being accused of. The relevant building regulation were read aloud; these stated that the ventilation of an indoor garage located at a production facility should have sensors that would detect high concentrations of toxic gas. The ventilation would then be triggered and expel the poisonous fumes. It had seemed like a long wait but I knew now what I faced.

Ventilation had been included in the design, but it was triggered manually; building regulations had been violated with grave consequences, and as chief project engineer I was responsible. But there were others who were also responsible and they were nowhere to be seen.

"What time am I looking at here?" I quietly asked the head lawyer, who was sitting next to me.

"Five years if you're lucky," he replied coldly. The man was a professional and had no sympathy for me.

The tension increased. I asked quietly for the opportunity to look at the building regulation. As I read, a ray of hope flickered through my mind; this regulation was not from the main body of building standards, it was a supplementary standard issued subsequently. I looked at the date it had been incorporated in building guidance before opening the documents for our design with trembling hands. The project design had been endorsed three days before the supplementary regulation had been issued. Thoughts flashed rapidly through my mind. *At that point the contract for supervising the design was not concluded. The corrections to the design proposed by the client had not been received. Our institute did not perform the role of client on this design. Yes, this shell has flown past and exploded close by but not right on top of me.*

I relaxed and waited for the presentations to conclude and then requested a word and spoke initially at a tangent to the main case. I expressed surprise that no one had spoken in my defence and that people I knew well had ascribed responsibility to me and wanted the material handing over to the prosecutor so a criminal case could be opened. I laid out my defence pretty coolly.

"That's interesting," the minister said, "very interesting. Well, what's the heart of the matter?"

I laid out my arguments regarding 'the heart of the matter'.

"So this means you're not guilty," said the minister, "then who is?"

"Judge not lest ye should be judged," I replied cheerfully, "the facility's operations are complex and anything could happen there." Again, I blurted out too much, "And it wasn't the worst death, he died in the arms of the woman he loved." I heard some restrained laughter which was quelled by the severe gaze of those in charge.

"Well, okay," said the minister, deciding to show

clemency, "get on with your life. Particularly since it's New Year next week. Consider it a New Year's gift. And you are also terrific," he said, looking at the specialists who had produced the case report, "dick-heads." Then he continued in a business-like manner, "Two weeks after the New Year, make some corrections to the design and supervise their implementation in situ."

"Could we make it three weeks?"

"What, don't you have time in two weeks?"

"Yes, but the thing is, I have a trip to the Caucasus booked right after the holidays. It's only ten days, so if I return right after that…"

"What's this 'if I return'?" roared the minister, but then he halted abruptly and said, "Great, three weeks then, but watch out for me." He turned his back on me. I think he was afraid of laughing and ruining the image he had cultivated over many years.

We poured into the corridor, we were all friends now, they slapped me on the back and offered to ply me with drinks in the evening before I headed to the Kursk station and went home.

No one mentioned the episode when I returned and I was not asked for a report. A kind of conspiracy of silence surrounded the affair. One week later I was in the Caucasus. Ten days later I implemented the minster's directive, completing it within two weeks. The case was closed forever.

Point B had not come upon me, or rather it had but only as a transition and not a conclusion. Thank goodness.

We did all the usual stuff in the Caucasus, traversed the mountain gorges and skied; we also had to undertake something that was not usual, a rescue operation when one of our party was injured. We took it in turns to carry the stretcher with the wounded climber, who was lain in a sleeping bag, fastened to it. We were in a rush because we were afraid that he would freeze to death. When we finally reached the district hospital in

Tyrnyauz it transpired that he needed blood, but it had to be group O rhesus positive. We shared the same blood type, so I provided almost two tumblers of blood to save his life.

We got home safely and forgot about this episode, but I realised later that this was a Point A in my life. Point B came one year later in very unusual circumstances.

In 1980, my working arrangements changed when I was appointed head of the economics department. I wondered if this might be a poisoned chalice because, for some reason, no one had held the post for longer than two months. I had no experience of economics before and had not dealt seriously with these disciplines at the institute because up until then I could not have imagined having such an appointment. I wondered if there was another possibility here. Perhaps I had been appointed to ensure there was a distance between the board and any economic consequences. You know that some people do not like to be told the truth and many do not like to have any responsibilities. Well, as the proverb states, 'No good deed goes unpunished'. Perhaps some people hoped I would crash and burn soon, like those before me, and therefore get my comeuppance.

Nevertheless, I soon acquired an understanding of this new area and found it to be no harder than dealing with engineering problems. However, my lack of formal economics education meant some colleagues would make insinuations about my lack of training whenever we dealt with an issue. I began to think about how to address this and acquire an economics education with the desired swiftness. I started to turn my eyes to the centres of economic thinking in the Soviet Union; the most important of these was the Lomonosov Moscow State University.

I took advantage of a routine working visit to the Ministry of Fuel and Gas Industries in the summer of 1981 and paid them a visit. There was no guard on the door so I roamed freely along the endless corridors of the Faculty of Economics, looking at the names of departments and laboratories. One plaque inscribed with the words *The Department of the Organisation and Management of Social Production* caught my attention. I felt this was close to what I wanted. I knew something about the area of production management and could execute it effectively. I opened the door warily and looked inside. There was only one person inside the large room, he was middle aged, burly, had close-cropped, grey hair and wore a suede jacket. He sat at a desk in the corner of the room and wrote something.

"You have come to see someone?" he said amiably.

"Yes, but I don't know about what exactly," I said, and outlined the problem.

"Why go all the way back to the beginning, you should be fine on the graduation course. We take engineers into our faculty. You'll begin in three months."

He called his secretary, who swiftly provided me with the necessary documents. I was pretty stunned by the unusually quick solution to my problem and began preparing the paperwork for the course that very same day when I got home.

I must say that I already had one unsuccessful attempt to enter post-graduate education. Immediately after I left the army in 1971, I submitted my documents to my very own Odesa Electrotechnical Institute. I passed the specialist exam with flying colours. I had also passed exams in philosophy and English with flying colours while still in the army. I wrote an excellent essay and was completely confident of my success. However, the very next day, the head of the department, an old friend of my late father, asked me to see him.

"Boris," he said, "go back home, you won't be able to come here."

"Why not?" I asked indignantly, "I've ticked all the boxes."

"You won't get on the course," he reiterated, "all the free

places have already been taken. Find another place, somewhere," he added, averting his gaze.

The percentages, I thought that's what it is? I was seething inwardly, but kept my cool. Was this my country? The country for which I had repeatedly risked my health and my life? The country that keeps you on a short leash, and gives with one hand, while it takes away with the other.

"Well," I said, "this place isn't my only option," and departed with a stony smile.

No one asked me about it back home and I kept shtum. However, I developed an aversion to the specialty I had acquired at the institute , and swapped it for another one when the chance arose.

I lived, worked, successfully pursued an engineering career, but I never forgot that first unsuccessful experience. But now, ten years later, I had the opportunity to redeem myself, to prove to myself that I could succeed as a post-graduate, and finally forget about it.

My documents were submitted punctually and three months later I turned up to take the exams. I wore the Glavmorneftegaz uniform to strengthen my hand. It was blue and adorned with anchors, shiny buttons, epaulettes with fancy badges, and buttonholes. I was the equivalent of the highest rank of captain in the navy and wore three big, captain's stars. The uniform made quite an impression on the girls and police that I encountered. However, I did not know how they would take it in this 'ivory tower of dedication to science'. But why not give it a try.

"Oh, look at you," the head of the department said on meeting me. However, having read my surname on the form, he cooled noticeably towards me. "And what kind of uniform is this?" he asked suddenly. This question was posed by anyone who met me at university for the first time. But without waiting

[1] Glavmorneftegaz was the Soviet body responsible for developing offshore oil and gas fields

for an answer he fired off the second question which was also typical. "Tell me, why don't you try to enter the Moscow Institute of Transport Engineering?"

Moscow was rife with vague rumours about this institute. Apparently gaining entrance to that establishment depended solely on a candidate's level of knowledge. This renown led to the institute producing several brilliant graduates in various fields, from mathematics to economics. But what did that have to do with transport engineering? That was an enigma. I do not know the answer and I never write about things of which I have no knowledge.

"No," I replied firmly, "I'll come here, and if it doesn't work out, then that's just destiny."

"Well," the man who would be the future mayor of Moscow said portentously, "have a go," and shook his head.

Everything was much more complicated than I had thought. There were fifty-five applicants for five places. I was the sole engineer, the rest were generally chief economists in various enterprises. No one cared about my previously submitted candidate's exams. The subjects I studied now were completely unfamiliar. There was no numerical limit on the exams. They just had to be taken and submitted, until there were exactly as many of us remaining as there were seats. That is, five people. I went to the university library and asked for literature on the subject of the first exam, political economy. I was amazed at the number of books I was handed. However, when I began to read them at high speed it got easier. I learned it all very readily for some reason. The area of my brain responsible for this subject was as empty as that of a baby and ready to be filled. It helped that I was used to assimilating a lot of information as someone involved in engineering design.

The day of the exam came. The situation was akin to combat. The exam was taken by the choirmasters of economic science, the creators of socialist economy. The first five applicants failed then the sixth and seventh were 'satisfactory'.

I went in eighth place. "Draw a ticket with the questions," they said. I took the ticket, but did not turn it over because one of the examiners said to another, "We are only moving slowly, the exams are holding us up." Then they spoke to the crowd in the corridor, "Maybe somebody wants to go straight for an interview without a ticket with pro forma questions?"

"I want to," I said delightedly. "I haven't looked at the ticket yet. I'm happy with a free ranging interview."

"All right, young fellow."

The interview began. The first question was the usual, "What kind of uniform is this?"

"I know what the second question will be," I replied.

"So what will it be?" the examiner asked curiously.

"Why don't you go to the Moscow Institute of Transport Engineering?" I replied.

"Young man," the examiner said, being twenty years older than me, "you have yet to show you are worthy of this question." He asked a question on my specialty, then again another and another. We talked for about fifteen minutes.

He listened to my answers and frowned slightly when I tried to argue; I could not understand how he was evaluating my knowledge. It is worth saying that since I was in uniform, when I sat down I placed the cap with the gold braid and the badge with the anchor and the drilling rig on the table to my right. It was a dazzling bit of kit and the only thing I still have from this uniform.

The examiner looked at the glittering cap and then at me. He squinted suddenly, as if trying to remember something. "Tell me," he said, "have you ever been to the Elbrus area?"

"Oh yes," I answered, "I've been there every year for the past nine years."

"And were you there last January?"

"Yes, right after the New Year."

"I remember," the examiner replied quickly, "you were carrying a stretcher, at the front, right-hand side. I saw you hazily, as in a dream. And then I saw you just as hazily in the hospital when you donated blood. I'm still having a hard time walking." He looked at the stick with the handle and rubber tip leaning against the table behind which he sat.

We both fell silent. I felt awkward. "Maybe I should go to another examiner," I suggested quietly.

"You answered well enough," he retorted. "Let's get the score sheet." He quickly scored me and turned away.

I did not look at the student's record book until I got out. "How much did you get?" they asked, pouncing on me in the corridor.

"I'll look now," I replied, and turned the sheet over slowly.

"Terrific," the crowd of applicants breathed out in unison and in relief. "Well, old lad, you've done it."

"Yes, it's possible I have," I replied mechanically, and went to prepare for the next exam.

There were a many of them, an exam every three days. Finally, there were just five candidates left, and at the last exam they did not kick anyone out. Afterwards we all gathered at the faculty. The head looked grim. "Guys," he said, "they called us from the Party Committee. There is an accreditation commission tomorrow." Then he looked at me expressively.

"What is that?" everyone blurted out, "it's like a rude word."

However, there was nothing for it, and the next day we stood before the Party Committee of the Faculty of Economics.

I thought I might as well go first and get it over with and entered.

"Sit down."

I sat down.

"What kind of uniform is this?" asked the chairman of

the commission, who would be a future member of the State Emergency Committee. Something kept me from talking as before about the second question and I answered seriously. "So," he said and read aloud my name. Then, without looking at the form he said, "Are you a member of the Communist Party of the Soviet Union?"

"I am," I answered.

"Did you serve in the army?"

"I did."

"Do you have any awards?"

"I have some awards."

"And what kind of civic work do you undertake?"

This was my trump card. "I am the secretary of the Primary Party Organisation," I said loudly. It was the truth, but with one little refinement. Three months previously the Party Organisation of our institute was divided into nine smaller bodies. This restructure was probably to improve the reporting to the district Party Committee. As a result, I was elected, well in fact appointed, secretary of the Party's organisational management structure, and was the youngest there.

The blow hit home. "Boris Grigorevich," said the chairman, "leave us for a couple of minutes, we'll call you back in."

I turned and exited but noticed, out of the corner of my eye, a familiar face sitting at the side of the table.

"Well?" they asked me in the corridor.

"I don't know, they said they will call me back in."

The head of the department walked slowly along the corridor, looking at us reproachfully.

"Come in, sit down," they called me back again. The chairman stood up, cleared his throat and said with pathos, "We will recommend you." He added a little quieter, to his colleagues, "Feldman finishes this year, so we'll take him."

"Thank you," I said and left.

"Well?" the head of the department asked.

"They will recommend me to replace Feldman," I replied.

"Feldman isn't here anymore," the manager said dumbfounded. "However, it makes no difference now."

It really made no difference. There came the intermediate point B, which was point A in post-graduate school. As the ancients said with truth, 'And in the end there is a beginning'.

I enrolled as a post-graduate, completed my studies in four years and was the first in my group to defend a thesis in January 1986 at a meeting of the Academic Council of Moscow State University. A new point B had arrived, which was point A of the next stage of life.

At that time I was thinking a great deal about the principle of causation in our destiny. Where processes begin and are completed and their inter relationships. In real life, point A always precedes point B. In the relationship between a man and a woman, for example, point B may occur even before the appearance of point A. In the subtle world of human feelings, as well as in the quantum mechanics, there may be a violation of the causal principle: an effect may precede the cause. In this context, we all feel implicitly that point A is Yes, and point B is No. Remember, as the poet said:

I am like a train,
What has been running for so many years
Between the city of Yes
And the city of No.
My nerves are tense,
Like the wires,
Between the city of No
And the city of Yes![2]

Measure this idea for size against your own life and maybe it will suit you.

[2] Y.A. Yevtushenko "Two Cities" 1990

The phone rang abruptly and I picked up the receiver, only to find it was the ministry. "Where are we with the project?" the manager of the head office asked, "I am already being hassled by the minister."

It was mid-January 1990, only two weeks after the New Year, and work had already become demanding. "Yes, everything is okay," I replied, "and on schedule." I did not need anyone creating a problem for me. I would be in the Caucasus in a month, for my usual two-week winter holiday. There was an uproar at work and they might not let me take my leave.

"So what's okay about it?" he raged down the receiver. "Gipromorneft hasn't started work on the project yet. Are you the chief project engineer or what?"

It was true that work had not yet begun. By this point I had worked for four years as deputy research director at the institute, which undertook the responsibility for a number of offshore oil and gas fields. The most difficult of these concerned the development of a giant gas field in the Barents Sea, in an area that was subject to a dispute between the Soviet Union and Norway.

A group of international experts were working on the project, so, as the chief specialist who had some knowledge of English, I was designated project head during the feasibility study phase. In Russia it is called the GIP, which when translated from an obscene abbreviation into ordinary language equates to chief project engineer. I was not paid anymore for this title but it offered a few more prospects for career development. However, I knew I would soon be criticised if things were not going 'just so'. Our company was the general designer of the project, but there were numerous specialist sub-contractors; the Baku based institute, Gipromorneft, was one of them and their progress was slow despite being pressured by every means possible over the telephone.

I laid out the situation conscientiously before my agitated ministry boss. "What are you waiting for?" he barked angrily down the phone, "take some specialists with you and go there. Orientate yourself to the locality. Set off tomorrow."

In accord with the logic we lived by then he was quite right. "I'll fly out immediately of course," I replied.

'Tomorrow' did not come too swiftly, but on the nineteenth of January we landed at Baku airport, having flown via Moscow. I was accompanied by three experts from our institute. A white *RAFik* multi-person vehicle was waiting for us. We took our seats and exited on to the main road, which was deserted; only one police car passed. Something was not right. "Where are all the cars?" I asked the driver. He was an elderly Azerbaijani in a cap traditionally worn by airport employees. He remained silent and I wondered whether he had understood me.

We drove for about two kilometres and everywhere we went was just as deserted. Some traffic lights operated and while we were waiting at a red light I saw a small group of people at the junction. They approached the car while we were stationary and I saw they were young and were holding severed, metre-long pieces of metal armature. One of them said something in Azerbaijani and the driver turned off the engine. Another one of them, speaking Russian, told us they would check our documents and ordered us to get out of the car.

I felt that the situation was potentially very dangerous and looked at the driver. He sat motionlessly without looking at us. "What's going on?" my companions asked with some agitation, "what documents check?"

We got out of the vehicle.

"Are you Armenians?" asked the first man and looked at our passports.

The hell with that, I thought, but said aloud, "No, there

are no Armenians with us. We are from Crimea. We are on a business trip." I knew that two years ago there had been a big issue between the Armenians and Azerbaijanis in Sumgait. Not again, I thought, if that's so, our goose is cooked.

"What about him?" asked one of the Azerbaijanis, pointing at one of our experts, who was small, swarthy and dark-eyed; he did have a look of someone Armenian, but his surname was Russian.

"My mother was Moldavian," he replied, adding angrily, "and my grandmother was Jewish."

"We'll get to you and your relatives in turn," replied the man checking our documents, "you can go when we've finished with you."

He finished checking the documents while the taciturn driver started the car, and we drove along the deserted road; although I thought it would be better if we had turned back and caught the first available flight home; looking at my companions I realised that they were thinking the same.

Silence reigned until the car entered the city. What we saw there bore no resemblance to the pristine, neat and elegant Baku I had first visited in 1967 during a fourth year university field trip. At that time it was a fun environment inhabited by people of many nationalities. Apart from the Azerbaijanis, Armenians were the largest group, comprising one-third of the population; there were also Jews, Kurds and other, less numerous, ethnic groups. They lived amicably alongside each other, preserving their culture, singing their songs and visiting each other's homes.

I had visited with my friend who was on the same course, Yulyk, and we had stayed with some distant relatives of his while we were in the city. We had meandered around various, to us, exotic places and reached the conclusion that it was not a bad place to be. That is why when the allocations were underway for our fifth year we easily succumbed to an approach by a head-hunter from Azerbaijan's Ministry of Communications. If it had not been for the renowned escapade of the Soviet Union in 1968 (I was urgently conscripted into the army and forgot about the fifth year placement) I would have been living there now.

It was an extremely unwelcoming place now. There was debris on the streets, fragments of broken furniture; a muffled uproar and desperate cries sounded from somewhere in the distance. It seemed as if somewhere was on fire in the city and I could smell smoke and burning petrol. The driver dropped us off at the hotel where the woman behind the reception desk seemed surprised to see us but did not say anything about it. We settled in quickly, stashed our things in the hotel rooms, got back into the *RAFik*, which was waiting for us, and headed for work.

It looked even stranger at the Gipromorneft Institute. Many of the experts who had worked there had been Armenians, but I saw no one working there now. We headed for the management's office, the people there averted their eyes and said something about enemy plots, Nagorno Karabakh, and Stepanakert ... they spoke of refugees from these provinces and Armenia.

"Baku is very agitated right now," my colleague, the deputy director, a forty-five year old Azerbaijani, said, "there are a lot of incomers in the city and a lot of extremely unpleasant events may occur during the course of the next day. We have lost our best people right now."

So, that's why they haven't started work on our project, I thought, there was actually no one to start working on it. I said aloud, "Perhaps we could discuss this problem with the directors?"

The directors were situated in the Kaspmorneft association where we travelled via still-empty streets, leaving my colleagues at the institute. I wondered where all the people were until we drove around Lenin Square and I realised what was going on. A huge crowd had gathered there, I had never seen so many people together in one place, before or since. They were addressed from a rostrum and the crowd roared in response.

After five in the evening we arrived at the association. We also encountered chaos; both the security staff and the workers had disappeared. We walked through the corridors, the reception counter was closed and none of the organisation's deputies were at their desks. I suddenly saw something move in one of the offices and looked inside. A friend of mine, a senior functionary from a Soviet ministry, sat there in full admiral's uniform, which was optional. His area of responsibility was the country's oil and gas fleet.

"Come in," he said, "and make it a little less tedious."

We briefly discussed the situation, which by all accounts was bad. Nevertheless, we could not have imagined then just how bad it was. "It's nothing," said our admiral, "tomorrow I'll head for Astrakhan and 'bollocks to it', the ship is setting off then." He looked dubiously at the window and said, "Get out of this place if you can."

Loud noises came from outside, there were shouts and the sound of dozens of feet stamping through the corridors. I peered outside. A large crowd of youths armed with cudgels of all kinds were breaking into the unguarded building. The door was suddenly kicked open. We froze as a dozen or so heads peered around the doorframe. "Are there any Armenians here?" Followed by, "Bring them out here!"

The admiral rose from his desk and drew himself up to his full, outstanding height, with his shiny buttons, gold braid, officer's stripes and service ribbons, "There are no Armenians here," he boomed, "we're at work, simply at work."

I sensed the mob's mood becoming more neutral, perhaps more peaceful. The heads disappeared and the group of youths armed with clubs, sticks, hammers, and even axes, rushed off elsewhere, breaking into smaller groups. I got my breath back. That mob had been so close, but they had passed, for now.

I described my issue briefly to the admiral. "Go back to the institute," he said, "there is nothing for you to do here. There were some experts there."

"Yes, there really are 'some experts' here," the local deputy director said morosely, when I returned to the institute, "but they can't deal with this work now. You'll need to find another sub-contractor."

Meanwhile, the uproar and cries from the street had increased. I looked cautiously out of the window. A huge mass of people was pouring out of the square and through the streets. There were screams and cries, some vague and distant, in an indistinguishable cacophony. It seemed that people were being maimed and killed while we sat, unable to do anything. I became really frightened. Although I am not a timid person and would never usually be afraid to fight in an open conflict, it is quite another thing to feel like a hare harried by the hounds. I had a sense that the people around me felt the same way as we went on to the street.

The crowd had melted away, leaving debris and chaos in their wake. The *Volga* vehicle in which we had arrived had been flipped on its side and some liquid flowed from it. The driver was nowhere to be seen. I headed for the hotel on foot, bypassing heaped rubbish. Suddenly, there was a despairing cry from somewhere ahead of me; I looked in the direction of the noise and saw a man fall from a fifth floor window on to the asphalt fifty metres away from me. I was certain he had been thrown from the building. Even at that distance and in the dim light of dusk I could see a huge puddle of blood spreading around him. I rushed to a telephone booth and dialled for an ambulance. "All our ambulances are out on calls," the woman on the other end of the line replied. Then she cried suddenly,

"Yes, and there are no ambulances, no doctors too, nothing," and hung up.

I tried to telephone the police but no one picked up. I approached the body and could soon see that he was not breathing and was very obviously dead. There was absolutely no one else on the street. I could only move on. That's my hotel. Aha they're checking documents there too, the same merry gang armed with bits of metal. Luckily my colleagues will be in their rooms. We can leave no sooner than tomorrow and we'd better be off sharpish then, I thought.

It was already very late, the city was dark and all the lights were switched off. Something burned somewhere, but the noise began to subside. During this night, according to various, not always verified data, about one hundred and forty people were killed and over seven hundred were wounded. I learned subsequently that as a result of these events, five thousand people left the republic. It was, of course, impossible to sleep. At about two in the morning I heard the roar of engines and the sound of automatic weapons being fired. A column of vehicles and military equipment was passing through the city. I found out later that an army corps of approximately thirty-five thousand troops had entered Baku during the night of the nineteenth to twentieth of January. One of the divisions was commanded by Colonel Aleksandr Lebed, who would later become a renowned general.

When we went into the street the following morning we immediately encountered an armed patrol commanded by a thirty-five year old officer with a captain's epaulettes. I spoke for everyone, "We're not locals, we've come from Crimea on a business trip and we're leaving tomorrow."

"You're from Crimea?" said the officer removing his cap and looking closer at me. "I know you," he said suddenly switching to the familiar form of 'you', "do you remember the nature reserve in Yalta? I'd just returned from Afghanistan.

Myself and a marine division were allocated for guarding the bosses. Leonid Ilyich Brezhnev was there on a 'friendly', to say it that way, visit, and we were in the outer cordon with a helicopter to boot. You came from nowhere. We chased you and you really put us through it."

It transpired that this was the same lieutenant who had run after us through the mountains a decade ago. He introduced himself as Artur, with an ordinary Armenian surname ending with 'ian' as they often do. I introduced myself too and we started chatting.

"Many people died today," he said sorrowfully, "the burial detail worked through the night. I have a problem, my wife is six months pregnant and she's hiding in the barracks. She can't venture into the city or she'll be killed."

"They'd kill a pregnant woman," I said in astonishment, "what have we come to?"

"Yes," he stated firmly, "they'd kill a pregnant woman too." Then he asked unexpectedly, "Maybe you could take her with you. She has relatives in Mariupol and there's no other way of getting out of here right now."

"Does she have a ticket?"

"What ticket? There is nothing. There's just me and martial law."

"Listen, I don't have much of a chance to help you. I'm struggling to get out of this hell hole myself." Then an unexpected thought entered my head and Artur noticed a change in my expression.

"What," he asked, "what is it?"

"Let's meet up after lunch, I don't want to encourage false hope but there is possibly another option." I remembered my suddenly interrupted conversation with the admiral yesterday during which a supply ship had been mentioned. It was heading for a construction plant in Astrakhan tonight, bearing items for offshore platforms. You would not, of course, usually send a pregnant woman on board such a ship but I could berth one of my three specialists on the vessel. That would leave a free place on the plane. It was a sound idea and in the evening we stuck our engineer on that ship as part of the maintenance team. He had no creature comforts but he was prepared to make the sacrifice.

"You'll go to the construction plant and then return home by train," I said, and the issue was decided.

Artur brought his wife to the airport the following day. Three soldiers armed with *Kalashnikovs* sat alongside him in the *UAZ* military vehicle, which resembled a *Land Rover*. We entered the airport terminal and approached the counter.

"The man this ticket was bought for is no longer flying. Please transfer it to this woman."

The woman serving behind the counter shook her head. Artur flushed angrily but said nothing. His wife raised both hands and took off the gold chain she wore around her neck. The woman shook her head again. Artur's wife placed a ring with a red stone next to the chain. The woman shook her head again. It was joined by an engagement ring.

"OK," said the woman, "enter." She whispered something to a man standing next to her in aviation uniform.

Ultimately, we flew with Artur's wife to Moscow and parted from her, having supplied her with some money for the rest of her trip. It was only thirty roubles, but that was enough money to help her in those days.

After this nightmare I understood with absolute clarity that our previous simple and relatively poor but comfortable world had vanished without a trace. All the subsequent changes life threw at me did not cause me too much of a surprise. I could rest on this understanding, but, as with many people I have met throughout my life, there is another twist in the tale.

During April 2000 I went to a conference in Dnipropetrovsk. I was late so my driver floored the accelerator and our *BMW* travelled at well above the speed limit. We were spotted by the traffic police and pulled over at Melitopol. The police officer was preparing to issue the maximum legal penalty against us. I knew we would need to pay the fine quickly and get off.

"Comrade Major, I'm ready to pay the fine for speeding but I'm in a rush. Could you sort it out as soon as possible?"

He raised his head and looked at me. It was Artur. He was older now and had a scar on his forehead, but he was clearly recognisable.

"How are you and where did you get the scar from?" I asked.

"Karabakh."

"What about your wife and child?"

"My son is now ten years old."

"So is everything fine now?"

"Yes, everything's fine," replied Artur. "Okay, on you way, and don't break the speed limit again. You're running as always."

"And you're chasing as always. What about the fine?"

"I'll pay," said Artur, "I'm obliged to you if you remember?"

We parted I think forever now, but if we ever meet again I will be sure to let you know.

The New Era, or War is War

An irritatingly loud noise tore me from the embrace of sleep. At first I wondered if it was the alarm clock and laboriously raised my head from the pillow to check the time. It was three in the morning and I had only been in bed for half an hour. I realised the telephone was ringing and wondered who might be impatient enough to telephone at this time. I picked up the receiver and barked, Yes, into the mouthpiece.

"Hello, I'm sorry for ringing so late but you need to come into work immediately." It was my deputy and between us we ran one of the largest banks in Crimea.

"What's happened?" I asked him.

"I don't want to say on the phone, but come and see for yourself. We are a little exploded here."

My drowsiness dispersed immediately and ten minutes later I was rumbling along the dark streets in my company *Volga*. I reached the bank and was shocked by the scene that met me. The windows were shattered and fragments of various debris littered the pavement. It was even worse inside. The false ceiling had collapsed on to the computers. The metal door of the vault was blown off its hinges and had landed at the end of the corridor near where the duty police officer stood on guard. There were, thank God, no casualties but the place was certainly pretty destroyed. In spite of the late hour there was a crowd of onlookers and the police were already making enquiries.

"The bank robber reached the windowsill from the street outside the building and threw a triton block against the glass, which broke it. The alarm went off and this was immediately followed by an explosion," the inspector said. "Do you suspect anyone?"

I did not suspect anyone, after all I had only been the bank manager for two weeks and had not had time to make enemies. There was another manager before me who had left with a bit of a stink, but that had nothing to do with me.

I knew I needed to do something and started telephoning people. By six in the morning the entire management team was at work. Thankfully, I managed not to be affected by the tragic aspect of the situation, instead I remembered some old cartoons from the Soviet era: The German king gave our Tsar the finger and then declared war on him. And our Tsar, red nosed and with a shovel of a beard gave a speech to the troops. "Soldiers, they gave the finger to your Tsar, we will fight them to the death!"

I wondered who had given us the finger and decided to address the team, but I did not deviate far from the example set by the cartoon hero. "Friends," I said, "someone has decided to intimidate us. They have attacked us and we are able to give a fitting reply."

Weirdly, my unusual speech had an impact on people, the staff were now a united team; both those who had worked there a long time and the newer ones. They were waiting for a leader and when the balloon went up it rallied us all. People's eyes lit up and they heard the sound of the pipes leading them into battle. I was forced to become a crisis manager and enjoyed the challenge. I remain a crisis manager to this day; there are always enough crises.

During the morning, glaziers, builders and cleaners worked away. The main bulk of the debris was cleared by lunchtime. I went home for a bite to eat in the ninth storey apartment building where I was living. As I was driving across the junction with Kyivska Street in the city centre, someone fired, just once, at my car. The bullet passed through the windshield and between the driver and security guard in the front seats; it narrowly missed my right ear as it went through the rear window. No one was injured but, not surprisingly, it had quite an effect on us. We were very lucky really.

The driver pulled up to the kerb and stopped the car; in his eagerness to leave us he almost crashed into a tree. He opened the door, yelled and ran off; I did not see him again. The guard froze and remained silent; I did not hear him speak again that day. I fell immediately into a state of violent exaltation, gripped only by the thought that when in battle you fight back. We were unarmed, but it did not stop me. I immediately took the driver's place, floored the accelerator, swung the car around and speed off in pursuit of the crooks. I'll chase and catch them and smack 'em down into the gutter, was the thought stirring within me. But there was no chance because driving quickly in a car with broken windows is impossible, the air streamed in, I struggled to see clearly and soon lost sight of the car I was chasing.

There was nothing to be done, I turned the car around and went home for my lunch; my terrified guard was still sitting on my right. With all this hassle we were running half an hour late and his wife was standing on the balcony ready to give me a piece of her mind about this lack of punctuality, but she was struck dumb when she saw our tensed faces and the car with the smashed windscreen.

I telephoned the bank from home and reported the incident. A new driver arrived, along with the man responsible for security. He tutted, touched the remaining shattered glass, which was still hanging where the windscreen had been, and left.

I realised that someone had declared war on us. There was no sense in waiting for help from anywhere. I remembered Aleksandr the Third's saying that Russia has only two allies: its army and its navy. Well, okay, I would create an army. Two hours later we were recruiting new staff from the many unemployed people who were hanging around on the streets; ex-athletes and military, and other people without any qualifications. We found experienced military officers in the existing team and eventually we assembled about twenty people and spent time on some training sessions with this motley crew. I realise now that this was useless in practical terms, but it did help us to stop feeling like hares pursued by hounds. Senior personnel of the bank were escorted to and from work and we introduced some secure areas in the bank itself. I began travelling in an escorted vehicle, and there were armed guards.

A new driver was found; he came, sat in his place and started work. He said nothing and was afraid of no one. He worked with me for about fourteen years before moving to another organisation. He was a regular man with his plusses and minuses, but the bravery he showed in the situation we faced was highly regarded by those around him.

Not surprisingly, our activities did not fail to attract attention. Various odd bods swirled around us with various proposals. "If you pay us, we'll sort it all out," one said. Another said, "Let us sell you something useful in this situation."

One instance was especially interesting and characteristic of these offers. An unknown man came from off the street to see me; "I heard you have a problem," he said. The whole scenario then became like a scene from Zhvanetskyi's satirical writing.

"Well, what is it?" I asked.

"I have something inexpensive to offer you."

"What?"

In reply he handed me a piece of paper with details of the tactical capability and technical data of a Strela 2M MANPAD.

"Are you out of your mind? What on earth would we do with that, are we an anti-aircraft division? Why would we need protecting from aircraft?"

"Who knows, it might be useful against things that don't fly," hissed my visitor.

"You know what, take yourself back to the mad house or I'll phone the police."

"Well, if that's what you want," he said and disappeared.

Half an hour later, two strangers came to see me with wan smiles and showed their IDs. "You've been offered a Strela

2M?" they asked, already knowing the answer.

"A nutter offered me one." I wondered how they knew this. "Are you from the same funny farm as him?"

"That's unfortunate," they chorused and became very sombre before also disappearing without a trace. That was that.

At this point I again wondered what all this meant, who was responsible, where they were, and most importantly, why they had started attacking the bank and its staff. The police never appeared nor did they answer their telephone, and generally acted as if it had nothing to do with them.

I started asking the staff to check credit and deposit liabilities and resigned myself to considering a few possibilities. These were that someone clearly wanted to demonstrate something. But I did not know who or why. All these actions were clearly intended to flag up something. Apparently we were meant to work it out for ourselves.

I began to have certain suspicions and slowly crafted a working version. I had inherited a portfolio of dubious quality from the old manager. When I began in post I studied it and noted a number of indirectly connected loans issued at very low rates, which disadvantaged the bank. I had naturally demanded that the debtors return the finance issued or agree to renew the loans on different terms. The head of the enterprise concerned, let us say, the overall borrower, acted very oddly during negotiations; as if he wanted to threaten or perhaps warn us in some way. That's it, I decided, they're trying to pressure us. I demanded further negotiations and used them to regain control of the situation.

"It's not us," he said, "the credits are nothing really and you have no evidence." However, sensing that the situation was volatile, he added, "But if you will allow us two months to repay the loans and stop insisting on your version of events, I'll reimburse you for all damages and losses."

His proposal satisfied me on the whole. A 'bad peace'

without losses was better than 'a good squabble'. I well understood that we were not prepared for a full scale war so I decided to take him up on his offer. We repaired and renovated the building, they paid us everything back in time and we were all satisfied.

Six months later I resigned from the bank with their agreement and began a new life. The hassles I had experienced there were a baptism of fire and, of course, were imprinted in my memory. For a long while afterwards I occasionally bumped into the director of the company with whom I had made the deal. Every time we met, we looked at each other 'meaningfully'. These somewhat serious events had linked us inseparably together. Then one day he disappeared. Rumour had it that he had moved his business to Russia and got lost within its vast expanses. Time passed and eventually a decade had gone by and the events recounted above were ancient history.

The events could have been concluded there were it not for one more episode. I was skiing in Switzerland five years ago and chanced to meet an old friend who had once worked near that bank. He had emigrated long ago and nothing now tied him to Ukraine. We shared a drink at a bar situated plumb on the mountainside and were getting ready to go our separate ways when he said, "Do you remember those strange events at the bank?"

"Obviously I remember them."

"Do you understand what it was all about?"

"Of course, they reimbursed us for our losses and repaid the money."

"Yes, but those guys basically weren't to blame."

"Why not? They didn't object to paying us back."

"That doesn't mean anything, they'd needed the money and your losses were less than the profits they were going to acquire while increasing their authority at someone else's expense."

"Why at someone else's expense? Who is guilty?"

"Guilty?" He gave me a crafty glance. "There was a guy you once humiliated when he was in a certain job. He was avenging himself on you. Then he got frightened and scarpered without leaving a trace behind."

"Where did you get this information from?"

"From the man himself; we used to drink and chat occasionally."

"And the shot at the vehicle, was that also him?"

"I don't know anything about the shooting, you'll have to look elsewhere for an answer to that question."

There was no point looking into it sixteen years later. Pretty much anything happened mysteriously and incomprehensibly in those distant years and troubled times. Forget it you say to yourself, live and enjoy life. But I still regret that I was unable to catch up with the car from which someone had shot at me. You experience weird feelings at moments like that. Pushkin commented notably on this in his 'Little Tragedies':

All, all that threatens is with death
Conceals for the mortal heart
An ineffable delight…
Immortality may be secured
And happy is he who amid life's agitation
Can acquire and guide it now!

He said this after being fatally wounded in a duel on the Chernaya river two days earlier. However, I probably experienced 'rapture in battle at the edge of the dark abyss'. It is very, very dangerous to touch eternity.

The day began strangely with a bit of a furore. The day before yesterday, one of our corporate clients had instructed the bank to undertake a large transfer payment. He told us it was an advance payment for a large petrol tanker that was due to arrive in Sevastopol. The tanker's fuel would supply the fleet and would also be for sale on the open market. The payment scheme was excessively complicated in my view because the money originated from various sources and had accumulated in accounts held at our bank. Several payments were directed towards a Russian company that was paying for the fuel via its own bank account. I told the client's representative bluntly that I did not like the way the payment was being made through an intermediary but he assured me that I had nothing to worry about because it was all controlled by his company.

The owner of the company was a proper gentleman. Moreover, the payment did not utilise our credit facilities, although banks were involved in the transfer of the cash. This intimated that the credits could be combined into a single lump-sum payment. The first three transactions went through okay, and under the delivery terms stipulated the tanker was regarded as the property of the buyer immediately after it emerged from a Mediterranean port.

We were waiting for a nod from the buyer to enact the final payment after the vessel berthed at the port in Sevastopol, but it never came. Instead the company supplying the tanker called us. They said the tanker had been at the port for a long time and that the third and fourth payments had failed. It is not uncommon to encounter hiccups like this, the initial phase of the development of banking in Ukraine was accompanied by a high risk of default. Nowadays, these operations are carried out through letters of credit with payments made between the banks, and with the banks covering all the risks. Back then, however, everything depended utterly on the honesty and integrity of the contracting parties, therefore intermediaries were needed. Each of the contractors tried to control the settlement process in their own interest. The individual calling from the company struck a sharp and serious tone as he said, "If this is down to you, watch out."

"Who do you represent?" I asked.

He replied very clearly, and added, "The petrol is already utilised and apparently half the payment we are due won't ever arrive. What's more, the buyer isn't replying to our calls."

"Listen," I said, "the payment and delivery stuff is your business. They have nothing to do with the bank. We were instructed to carry out three payments and we carried out that instruction. As for the rest, sort it out between yourselves."

"Two," he replied, "only two payments, even if I believe everything else you've said."

"But you chose to receive payment through an intermediary, we're not a party to the contract. We have made three payments."

"Prove it, present the documents and we will check where the payment is being held up, otherwise we will assume that you are the guilty party."

If this had been a normal situation I would not have continued our conversation, but I knew it was extremely dangerous. To begin with there was the large scale of the tranche. Secondly, the client concerned, the buyer, was not responding to any form of communication. Thirdly, the caller had told me the real name of the company who had not received the payment from the Russian side. They were a company who would go to war if we could not prove we were innocent of this scam.

"Come," said the voice on the telephone from Moscow, "grab the payment documentation and come. We can deal with this quickly."

I did not think about it for too long. As a rule I usually

think quickly when I am in danger. There was a risk in going to Moscow, but an even bigger risk in not being proactive. "OK," I said, "I'll fly out tomorrow."

No sooner said than done and I arrived at Vnukovo Airport in Moscow on the morning of the following day, where an entourage was waiting for me. An hour later I entered a hotel situated on one of the capital city's main avenues, where it was rumoured that a 'very serious organisation' was based. I ascended to the relevant floor with my escort who never let me out of his sight; a fact which gave me pause for thought.

"Hold on a moment," said the secretary on the 'serious organisation's' reception, "the previous visitors are just about to leave."

We turned back into the corridor and saw there was another reception room nearby, much larger than the one we had just come out of. Its door opened unexpectedly and a man with a shaved head emerged, accompanied by two burly young men in black leather jackets. He must have been a tough guy once but was running to fat a little and now needed bodyguards. He looked around and then stared at us. His eyes fixed on us. Then the secretary peeked out of the reception we were visiting and told us to come in.

There were two well-dressed young people waiting inside. I talked with them and they looked through the payment documentation.

"Where are the originals?" one of them asked.

"I'm sorry," I replied, "the original have to remain with us. However, I personally vouch for the authenticity of the copies."

Fifteen minutes later and they had seemingly made up their minds. "Well," said the one who, judging by their appearance and conduct, was the senior official, "we have no issues with you. Leave a copy and you are free to go. You have a lift?"

"No," I replied, "I'm on my own." A sudden thought occurred to me. "Tell me," I said, "who is that strong looking guy with the shaved head who popped out of the reception nearby."

"You mean Vasyl Ivanovich?" I heard in reply, "he's the head of security here. Do you know him?"

I felt as if the spectres of the past were coming back to life. Kara Kum, 1969, the training camp. We had parted on bad terms, so bad you would not believe it. It would be better to avoid bumping into him on his own turf.

"Apparently not," I replied and went into the corridor.

Vasyl Ivanovich was standing in the same place as before, it was obvious he was waiting for me. He looked me in the eye again and recognised me. At this point a large group of people passed along the corridor. I pressed the elevator button to descend. The group were also standing by the elevators. Vasyl gave me a baleful glance and turned away sharply, rushing with his men towards the stairs.

I knew he wanted to catch me on the bottom floor so I pressed the elevator button to go up and while the crowd was cramming into the other lift I headed for the top floor alone. I climbed a short flight of stairs there and found myself in front of a door leading to the roof. It was hasped and padlocked. I sized it up and kicked it sharply. The padlock and hasps flew off and I was able to open it. I climbed swiftly on to the hotel's flat roof and headed for another doorway, which was also fitted with a padlock, but this time from the outside. They were probably fitted by the same locksmith who was too lazy to go to the top of the hotel twice. I picked up a piece of rebar lying nearby and twisted off the padlock easily. I took the elevator down, quickly ran through the passage and planted myself in the first available taxi idling by the sidewalk. I glanced back and noticed Vasyl also running out of the passage with his two young bullocks, who were gasping for breath. He was waving his hand in the air, it held something that glittered, but we were already pulling away from them.

"Kursk station please," I said to the driver.

When we arrived I paid the driver and when he was out of sight I took another taxi, this time to Kyiv station. The metro from there linked with Vnukovo Airport. I took the next flight from there to Sevastopol without any hassle. I figured that the experienced Vasyl would ask the driver where he had dropped me when the taxi returned to its place outside the hotel. Then he would hurtle towards Kursk station where he would look for me.

Something told me the tale of our unhappy relationship was not yet at an end. Twenty-six years had passed since we had first met and Vasyl Ivanovich had not forgotten or forgiven me. Now, of course, he would have every opportunity to repay me in a violent manner. The press had covered the assaults on the bank. If he arranged an attack on me no one would notice against the backdrop of violence directed against me by the organisation. People would assume that it was the organisation rather than my disgruntled ex-martial arts instructor if anything happened to me.

I was met at the airport in Sevastopol by one of the bank's guards and escorted to work safely. I had telephoned the bank before leaving Moscow; mobile telecommunications were already operating in those days, but they were huge with vast antenna.

I understood that the guard at the bank was unsuitable for dealing with something like this and so a couple of days later I met with an old friend, a sturdy police chief, and laid out the situation for him. He reacted calmly at first. "Okay," he said, "it was a long time ago, he isn't going to bother about avenging himself for some old grudge." However, when he learned the real name of the organisation he led was the "Spetsnaz" he took it seriously. "Okay, let's meet tomorrow, I'll gather some information. You lay low until tomorrow."

The following day when I arrived to meet my old friend and special police services commander, he was already waiting for me in his reception. "I've checked out your guy through my own channels. Some interesting characters from there are hanging around here. Let me set you up with my own guards in case, you never know what might happen."

A young special police officer with an automatic weapon was assigned to me; initially for a couple of days, then for a couple more. We began travelling around like characters in a spy movie, in three cars with armed guards.

The situation stabilised but the danger did not disappear, we were in a kind of stalemate. Two months later I opened a fresh issue of the *Kommersant* newspaper and checked out the section chronicling criminal activity. It reported a car bombing in Moscow. One of the victims who had been inside the vehicle was one of the leaders of a notorious organisation. The head of their security had been sitting alongside him. *Vasyl Ivanovich your dangerous habits didn't bring you to a good end. Or maybe this was an echo from the affair with the payments for the tanker? Or even some other dodgy business? I don't know I'm not an expert in the field of criminal feuds.*

The 'client' who had taken out a contract on me was gone and his order 'self-destructed'. The urgent need for an armed guard decreased, but I still considered it necessary and they liked it at the bank. The man who came to us first still works there. He completed university, left the police, took his pension, became a young granddad and still kept working quite successfully at the bank.

Perfection is the Enemy of the Good

"Take me home to Crimea," I said to the driver as I sat in the car.

It was September 2008. The day before, on Saturday, I had arrived at the fortieth anniversary event for alumni of the communications institute where I had studied. I was leaving with some relief; it is not too pleasant to observe how age changes the people you knew, objects and events. It is less complex when it comes to how you regard yourself; you look in the mirror every day and do not notice the small changes that occur day by day. You get used to them. However, looking at a classmate for the first time after forty years is a very different matter. No, I would rather turn away in blissful ignorance.

The car set off and I looked at my watch; it was two in the afternoon and I would be home by eight. At this point I remembered the basement apartment where I had lived with my distant relatives when I was at college. "Wait," I said to the driver, "we'll go along Velyka Arnautska Street before we head home."

Ten minutes later we were there. The car stopped opposite the building where I had lodged during my time at the institute. Thank God people no longer live in basements. They are usually occupied by bars now. The one I had lived in was a pharmacy.

I got out of the car and slowly retraced my well-walked route across the old Odesa district to the institute. Before and after the revolution the area had mainly been occupied by the Jewish proletariat. Some of the residential buildings were patched up here and there, however, the overall architecture had hardly changed. People were sitting on stools near some of the gateways; someone was playing dominoes, someone was languidly discussing the latest news.

It was here that I had once started a small tutoring

business. Now I remembered almost every residential building, the toilets in the yards, the vicious dogs, and of course my peers. I taught them the basics of school science, mainly, of course, mathematics when I was finishing my first year at the institute. I had not at that point forgotten the knowledge taught to me by my best teacher, my mother. In fact I still think I remember everything I learned from her, so she must have been a great teacher.

I remembered that the residential building I was standing next to was where Sema, the tailor's apprentice, had lived. I sorted out his work in the tenth class at my evening school. He had big ambitions, he wanted to go to college and eventually run his own sewing studio. I had once ordered a pair of fashionable slacks from him. My lessons cost one rouble a time, but tailoring the trousers and the material cost fifteen. I felt the bill did not favour me but he would not give way. Nevertheless, he created some chic pants, tight fitting higher up and then flaring, as the standards of the day required.

"I need to check the theoretical knowledge I gained from you by putting it to a practical test," he would say when I tried to haggle with him. Sema was totally uneducated but very sharp as far as I could see. "When I'm the director of a sewing studio," he would dream out loud in my presence, "then the cash will flow in."

I had grown up in an intellectual environment and therefore tried to persuade him to approach his dreams differently. "Set yourself small goals," I said.

"Why small?" he responded indignantly, "this is the best ambition I can both conceive of and achieve."

"Perfection is the enemy of good," I continued fervently.

The diligent Sema spent a long time working out what I was talking about and then disagreed. "If you always choose perfection, you'll get good things. And if you wait for that good thing, life will pass you by."

So each of us stood by our own opinion.

I stepped closer to the building where there were two old men sitting on an old, saggy sofa. One was telling an anecdote to the other. "You see," he said, "there are two people who meet by chance on the street and one says to the other, 'Sir, I know you have a girl of marriageable age and I am prepared to propose my lovely grandson as her husband.' 'And who is he apart from your grandson?' the other replied. 'He's finished university and is now an engineer.' 'Well, we'll say no to him,' answered the would-be bride's grandfather, 'he is an engineer and we want a butcher at least.' 'What?' asked the first guy 'is she really that beautiful?'"

"It's an old anecdote, Semion Lvovich," the other old man replied sluggishly, "even back in those days."

"Old like you and me," replied the other man.

I drew closer and looked carefully at him. Over forty years had passed but it could be my old pal Sema. He was bald, paunchy and wrinkly now, but I thought it could be him.

"Please excuse me," I said to him, "a certain Semion lived hereabouts in 1963 and sewed pants to order."

"Not pants but slacks," the man corrected me, "I sewed pants later when my brother sent me the kit I needed to sew jeans."

"I'm sorry," I said, unable to hold back, "and what's the difference between pants and slacks?"

"Darts," he replied.

Yes, it was the same Sema. "Darts," he repeated, placing the accent on the last syllable of the Russian word for darts for some reason.

"And you Boris, do you still teach mathematics or have you moved on?" he asked unexpectedly. "Don't be shy, take a seat." He inched sideways freeing up a space for me opposite a hole in the settee from which one of its springs protruded menacingly.

Semion Lvovich was wearing rather grubby linen pants, a faded short sleeved shirt, and slippers on his bare feet. A poverty stricken old man, I thought, probably a pensioner. If we continue this chat it will only be depressing. However, curiosity got the better of me and I sat next to him.

"So, Sema, you still recognise me after all this time?"

"You've almost not changed at all," he replied optimistically, "just your hair … ta ta to it. But you had a crew cut back in 1963 anyway."

That was true, long hair had only become fashionable in later years. Now short hair was fashionable again but, you know, compulsorily so.

"Sema," I asked out of curiosity, "what are you up to now? You're not still sewing pants?"

"No," he shook his head, "my youngest grandson runs all that now. In my factory they sew anything you can imagine, any brand name to suit any taste. From two steps away you can't tell them from the genuine article."

"At your factory? You work there?"

"A lot of people work in my business, I don't run it all myself."

"You have a large scale business?" I was laboriously becoming aware of the comic aspects of our situation.

"I haven't calculated how big it is, but I don't have enough relatives to oversee it."

"Where are you selling your gear? On the market?"

"No, in shops. One is just on the corner opposite to where you lived. I've got another seven in the city. My niece, Riva, looks after them."

"You've eight shops." I was surprised, he was more successful than his shabby apperance suggested.

"Yes, and five more in other cities; some are pretty profitable. There could be more but I don't have enough resources."

"So, during all the years we haven't seen each other you created this retail network?"

"Well, no. I returned from the US ten years ago, I went there in 1978."

"Do you miss it?"

"Yeah, but not much, it got hot there."

"How?" I had not caught his drift.

"The state turned up the heat worse than the Soviets, they were wanting more and more. Then the Chinese…"

"What Chinese?" I said in total confusion, "and what did the US take from you, what the hell did you have to give them? You mean it didn't go well there?"

"No, not to begin with. It was a new place, I didn't know the language, no one needed you to sew any trousers, there were tailors coming out your arse over there, but after a couple of years we settled in and organised international trade."

"Who is we?"

"Well, Leshe, Moshe, Kolia and Yana were over there. You'll remember some of them. The thing was the Chinese were selling cheap clothes in the States, so we decided to make them even cheaper."

"How were you able to become more competitive even than the Chinese? I thought no one had previously managed to do that." Again I was surprised.

"You see," Sema launched into a detailed reply, "we imported our rags from central Asia. In Tashkent, our Jewish business people who worked underground in the era of the Soviet Union had some connections dating back to those times. It's cheaper to manufacture there, even than in China. And they sew on the same Chinese labels."

"What Chinese labels?"

"Well, no they're not Chinese really. They sew on any useful label: *Dolce and Gabana, Armani, Versace* and others. But you order them to make the product so it doesn't stand out particularly from those brands. The turnover was such that I hadn't enough dough to pay for all the 'protection' needed at the customs points. And the Chinese got in trouble along with us. They had problems. The squeeze was put on them, they had a lot of hassle. And when they checked out what was happening, well, it caused us a serious problem. Then the police…"

"What, the 'protection' didn't help you?"

"No, money alone isn't enough in the States to organise a cover up for this sort of business. And the Chinese had their own 'protection', and in the police too," he said morosely.

"Ah, you didn't pay taxes?"

"What fucking taxes?" Sema threw his hands in the air, "Where do you get your profit if you pay taxes? In short we had to come back and sort it all out from here."

"And you wound up the business?"

"No need, it still operates. I have a terminal at the port controlled by my eldest grandson."

"Sema," I looked at him intently, "there's something I don't understand. If you are what you say you are, what are we to make of you sitting here in slippers, without a car or bodyguard?"

"Without a bodyguard," said Sema perplexed, "I had them, useless bloodsuckers, until I put them to work selling my ice cream. Let them do something useful." He pointed to a stand opposite us from which a couple of dodgy looking burly chaps were selling ice cream and glancing occasionally at us.

"Ice cream is also part of your business?"

"Yes, I have a production line at the ice cream factory."

"Probably operate by your middle grandson," I suggested politely.

"It's operated by my granddaughter, she's a beauty and not yet wedded off. Do you have anyone in mind that might do for her?"

"What about the butcher?" I said, trying to make a joke

of it.

"You can have the butcher yourself," he snapped back, "I need a well-educated, experienced lawyer."

"So, instruct your personnel department to recruit one," I ribbed him.

"That's an idea," he said, looking at me with interest. "Do you want a drink?" He looked at his companion who had remained sitting silently alongside us. "Lev, get some drinks out of the fridge."

Lev rose and disappeared, opening and closing the gate leading to the courtyard.

"Do you still live here?"

"No, I have a car there and Lev is my driver."

Lev returned with two misted bottles of beer. A black Range Rover, which occupied half the yard, was visible through the now open gate behind him.

"Hi Sema," said a tall, burly man walking past with a bag full of shopping.

"That's Moshe," said Sema, nodding at me, "he played billiards at the Topola."

I remembered Moshe, or Misha as we called him back then. He was a hustler, handsome, tall, slim and dark haired. He could play the piano, had amazing success with women and had never studied anywhere.

"He came back with me from America, he was also involved in the business, along with his children and grandchildren. He's changed since the old days."

"Sema," I said supping beer straight from the bottle, "what are you doing sitting like a pauper on this sofa?"

"I always come here on Sundays. I listen to people and catch up on the news. I grew up here if you remember. But what do you do? Do you teach?"

"No, I work in a bank, though I also occasionally teach a little."

"Like me, sometimes I sew a little. But about the bank; here I have a little stake in one."

"It's okay Sema, you don't have to explain anything to me. I guess you got everything you wanted in life."

"By the way Boris," he butted in, "you see Laura, Moshe's wife, waiting for him at the gate over there. I remember you were after her, but she gave herself to Moshe; its clear forty years have passed for her too."

I remembered a slim girl called Laura. She was the daughter of Motl the cobbler, and Clara, who was the main source of scandal on the street. The old folks I lodged with whispered to me that her parents had met in exile after serving their sentences, got acquainted, came together and then got hitched. Laura was a decent girl, a seamstress who had also attended my lessons. She really liked me and there was a point at which I really tried to pull her, but it was, as they said then on our street, an utter failure. "I'm a decent girl," Laura told me, "and will only give myself to my husband. And what kind of a husband would you be? You have to study for another five years. And what's more…"

Her stance had commanded respect and I became somewhat of a friend to her. When she first married a respectable retail employee I went to the wedding reception, which, as tradition dictated, was in the yard of her home.

I looked at her more closely. She had put on forty kilogrammes since I had last seen her and her face had become very similar to her mother's as I remembered it from all those years ago.

"Sema," I enquired, "is this her second marriage?"

"No, I came in between, but we weren't together for long."

He was silent. How many destinies, I thought, how many different destinies. Previously it had seemed to me that this quiet, almost small-town, life of Odesa was a like a swamp.

You could get bogged down in it and see all your plans and dreams buried in the mire. I tried to break free from traditional stereotypes, to acquire liberty and realise myself to the full. But time had passed and this view was not entirely, indeed not at all, true. You can probably realise yourself anywhere and always if you really want to. The atmosphere, the environment around you, does not play the most important role here.

"Listen Sema," I said, turning to him again, "do you remember our discussions about perfection being the enemy of the good?"

"Nothing bad will ever come of that which is better," said Sema philosophically.

"Okay, goodbye," I said, "we probably won't see each other again."

"Goodbye," he nodded, "it's always a pleasure to talk to an intelligent man. And as my late father said, 'any business from the fuck to the coffin should be completed sharpish and don't wait for the profit.'"

"You're just a poem made flesh."

"I often am, occasionally I am a poem."

"So, what became of the studying? Was I preparing you in vain for higher education? Did you make it to college?"

"No, I didn't have time." He continued with a quote from that famous Odesa anecdote, "And if I worked as a director of the sewing studio where Laura laboured as a seamstress, we probably would be together now."

"So that means you didn't have time to go to college?"

"Yeah, I manage fine without college." He was silent and then added, "You've got to concentrate on getting the cash in."

We said farewell cordially and I departed. It was four in the afternoon and I still had a six hour journey home before me. So much for Sema I thought, And I was trying to feel sorry for him. Well, time flies by as it must fly by. And I am also a physiognomist… but it seems the past has not disappeared but continues to live in the present. And then I remembered a poem by Andrei Dementyev:

Never regret anything after it has happened!
If it has occurred, you cannot change it,
Like a note from the past, crumpled with sadness
The last fragile thread torn away!

This verse really fits the situation; is perfection the enemy of the good or not? Finding no answer ready to hand I think that everyone has to answer this question for themselves.

A Woman is the Most Dangerous of Playthings…

The sunlit slope lay behind me. I turned around before the bottom station of the lift and took off my skis. The vast mountain loomed in front of me. That's a cool ski slope, almost half an hour of continuous descent, I thought. Up there on the plateau of Monte Rosa it was very cold with a piercing wind, but on the southern slope it was quite warm. The Italians parked vehicles over on their side, it was not possible to squeeze your way through; however, on the Swiss side all vehicles with internal combustion engines were prohibited. Everyone moved around on electric vehicles and the snow was pristine. On the Italian side the snow in the village had a black coating in places from the exhaust fumes, but it was still wonderful in the mountains.

I thought about these things as I approached the ski storage area. I had to descend about one hundred slippery steps on no-less slippery ski boots while shouldering the skis. I held the ski poles in my other hand just in case I slipped. I was more comfortable on skis, I was in my element on them, having glided the slopes for almost four decades, but on this descent I was having to take care not to flip on to my behind. I overcame this dangerous descent and pushed open the double doors that led into a large, noisy room. There were about two dozen people in there, their voices boomed through the smoky air with the room's unusually large echo. Two middle-aged women were smoking while they posed with their ski equipment.

"Boris," yelled one of them, placing the accent on the first syllable and then switching to English, "and where is Marko?" She accented the second syllable of his name.

They apparently knew a little of every language except Russian. However, the Russian words for great, thank you, goodbye and, of course, vodka they understood well enough. The Marko they referred to was my brother Mark. We, along with a small group of fellow skiers, had arrived in Cervinia three days ago. It was a nice town, an Italian ski resort with the highest altitude of two-thousand and fifty metres above sea level and the highest point for skiing on the Monte Rosa plateau at three and a half thousand metres. It was ringed by the magnificent mountains, the Monte Rosa, Brayhorn, Castor, and finally Switzerland's visiting card, the Matterhorn. It was possible to ascend and ski in your favourite of either country at that time as you pleased. I had visited Switzerland on many occasions, but now I had decided to try out the Italian side.

We were experienced skiers who rode the snow fast, sometimes crazily fast, and therefore relied on our own kit, however, it was about three hundred metres from our hotel to the ski lift. Everyone knows that skiers are a lazy tribe. It is not for nothing that they like to use ski lifts rather than clamber up the slopes. That was what the mountaineers always said when I was engaged in that kind of sport. The skiers said the same when I swapped over to their lazy sport. Anyway, we did not want to carry fifty kilograms of skis boots and poles around after breakfast, so we had picked a rented shack near the ski lift. Some chirpy local women made us welcome there in exchange for a modest fee. It was they who were now greeting us with their happy cries.

"Mark will be here later," I answered them in English. Mark and his friends were staying somewhere higher up in the mountains at a local restaurant. I had left them there because I wanted to visit a local ski shop before it closed; I had spotted some things I wanted to buy the previous day. I handed my outfit over to the locals, put on my 'civilian' boots and went out on to the main street, experiencing brief happiness at the transition from extreme tension to total relaxation. Anyone who undertakes any extreme sport will know this feeling. It is like the famous joke: a yogi takes one of his limbs, places it on a rock and bashes it with a hammer. "What's the pleasure in that?" asks a passing tourist; the yogi replies, "The pleasure is

140

when you miss."

When the hammer of fate avoided smashing us we were happy, but that was not always so. In 2012, the year this story is set, Mark broke his knee while skiing at high speed on the steep slopes of the French Avoriaz. He had twenty-five years' experience of skiing, but, alas, these accidents happen.

"Boris," someone said as they grabbed my sleeve from behind. I turned around.

"Sasha, how many years, how many winters has it been?"

It was Aleksandr, my old pal and now vice-chairman of one of the Ukrainian banks. We had not seen each other for ten years. Before that, during the era of the Soviet Union and after, we met annually when getting together in the Caucasian mountains or some other pleasant little spot. We greeted each other affectionately and walked on, swapping our impressions of the place. We checked out the ski shop then continued our stroll. Ultimately we decided to find a seat somewhere and celebrate our meeting with a few drinks. We sat on the veranda of one of the local bars and ordered a whisky, coffee and salad; then we drank, ordered some more drinks, then more.

"How long is it since we saw each other?" I asked.

"More than ten years," he replied and thought for a little while. "You know," he said, suddenly, "it's hard for me to assess those years. My material resources increased, but perhaps I lost something with regard to the moral scheme of things. Life was easier before. We lived in accordance with our desires, and since it was unlikely they would be completely realised, there was always a space left to dream. And our desires were simpler."

"Do you live according to your desires now?"

"Where possible, but my desires now often don't make sense. Time has turned everything around. Were it not for new possibilities that appeared I think I may have kept my first family. My daughters are adults, we rarely see each other, they're

141

probably hurt by what happened. I don't have children from the subsequent women and I am unlikely to have any."

"What subsequent women?" I asked with some surprise. "As I recollect having a few women running in 'parallel' was enough for you back then."

"That doesn't count," said Sasha, waving those parallel women away, "that was my childhood really and a child is allowed to indulge himself. Now it's something else. I can often obtain the fulfilment of my desires from a woman now. But I have nothing to do with it. They don't look at me, they aren't attracted by my personal qualities. It's business."

"Well, you said it, how old were you then? And now? And how old am I as well. So what's wrong with using your well-tried competitive edge?"

"Then," sighed Sasha, "I worked as chief engineer at a factory. I married while I was still at university and lived decently for a long time. Work, sport, family life. Remember how we traversed the Becho Pass?"

"Of course, and now we are ascending to above three and a half thousand metres every day, but not doing it ourselves really."

"That's just it," he muttered quietly and then continued, "life was flowing smoothly. Perhaps over time I would have become the director and then retired to be surrounded by my grateful children and grandchildren. But in 1992, a young specialist, joined the factory's management team. She was married with a child, but she and her husband were rumoured to be having problems. I was forty-two, but still as predatory as an eagle. She wore very short skirts, so when she carried papers to me in my office the hem of her skirt was above my desk. But she was seemingly innocent; that was until I had a business trip to the ministry in Moscow. I worked there for a couple of days, then Friday arrived and I couldn't leave because there were still some unresolved issues. Some additional information was

142

required and it was within the remit of our young specialist, Tanya. I rang the factory and reported back to the director. He told me he would send Tanya with the relevant documents so we could sort it quickly. She could explain it all to me in person. I agreed, thinking she would arrive on Sunday and we would go to the ministry on Monday. But no, she was there on the evening of the same day. She came to me in my room and I looked at her standing there with downcast eyes. Her thigh moved as if eager to do something. It caught my eye. I went to her and we clung to each other. I only came to my senses an hour and a half later. Then we made love again and again. She laughed and indulged her fantasies with me - And we still had Saturday and Sunday. Ahh, even now the memory sends shivers down my spine."

"So, was that the end of it?"

"Where could it go from there? We began to live a new life. She also had a family, a jealous husband and a baby. She was daring and inquisitive, so we met here and there occasionally; in hotels, in cars, at friends' places, in the great outdoors. Her relationship with her husband went completely sour and he headed off somewhere. He suspected something and tried to meet up with me before he left. That didn't happen, thank goodness. I began to see her regularly at her apartment but returned home to sleep. I gave the impression I was having to stay late at work, but my family life became more difficult. You'll understand this. After a couple of years of such a relationship situation this led to a final break with my wife, but that's another subject. Then the Soviet Union collapsed. The situation at the factory became extremely poor and I went solo. Initially I organised a small factory, using my own knowledge and experience. I dodged and weaved and got hold of my start-up capital. Then, as you know, I became a shareholder in the commercial bank where I still work. She also left the factory, rented a shop and embarked on the rag trade. Our relationship lasted but it moved to another level. I occasionally threw money at her and participated in her commercial operations. Sometimes I protected her from bandits. I was, overall, her senior comrade and her guardian."

"And what was this?"

"Sex or what do you mean? Sex continued at the rate of once a week. By then I'd married again and had another house."

"Again," I said in surprise and reflected aloud, "it's like in Bulgakov's writing where he says 'how he loved domesticated birds'."

"Yeah, yeah," said Sasha, nodding and continuing with the Bulgakov theme, "I took attractive girls under my wing. For a while everything was going well and stable enough. I had two wives."

Our chat had ceased being dull and I ordered another whisky. It would help me reflect on what he had said.

Sasha continued his tale. "Yes, I had a thought then, if I had two wives, couldn't I change them both? And the situation was favourable then. I received an interesting offer for the purchase of securities in several enterprises. The offer was initiated by an agency that lacked capital and so had turned to me. Their director was a bespectacled businesswoman in her thirties, a PhD candidate, dressed in a severe manner. However, I took a closer look at her and saw she had everything a woman should have. I always had a particular interest in women like her. I began to press her first from one angle, then another. She didn't seem to understand, then I invited her to my office at the weekend and she came. She remained unmoved until the last … and then I think she exceeded all my other women with the intensity of her passion, but she insisted everything had to be on a serious footing. No, we didn't need to get married but to act as if we were, operate according to schedule, give each other gifts, talk about love, and I had to provide serious support in her business. So you understand, I now had three wives. I'd never dreamed of that before. I was compelled to establish a schedule and employ a doctor to watch over my health, and munch on vitamin tablets."

"You poor thing," I said in an ironic, lamenting tone, "how did you have the time for all this, particularly since you need time just for the basic activities of living?"

"Yes, I said the same thing myself. But it was all right at the time. Then we were hit by the 1998 crisis. Everything went south, the hryvnia collapsed and there was no cash. Tanya went bankrupt and owed everyone money. I thought she might receive a slapping. The sum was pretty hefty and I thought about what to do. Katya, my other woman on the side, also went bankrupt. Securities tanked; their values sunk below the floor. The debts were so vast that I realised the situation was hopeless. Then my wife told me she was seeing someone else and filed for divorce. In short our triumvirate fell apart. Tanya's creditors were aware of our relationship and began to come to me, but I'd only just reached a decision and helped her out materially when she vanished along with my money, without paying her creditors. I worked it out eventually; it transpired her first husband had re-emerged and they had gone far away from all their previous hassles. Nothing more has been heard of them from that day forth. Then Katya started looking a little round. I asked if it was my baby. She explained it was not mine but hers and that she had a lawful husband and they were not getting divorced, but I could help out financially if I wanted. And the wife was on at me 'living together, mutual property'. Three months later I escaped the situation. I was as poor as a hawk in the forest, but I had no obligation. I stepped sideways from my life and decided to live like a monk. I worked for five years as if labouring under a curse. I renewed somethings, others I created from nothing. Now it's more tolerable, things have eased off."

"Are you here alone?"

"Yes, alone," he nodded, "but yesterday I met a woman

here."

"Don't worry, love will find you yet. Your lamentable experiences are no reason to be pessimistic. And you are largely to blame."

"Look who's talking," Sasha snapped at me, "look at yourself!" Then he added in a quieter voice, "I don't know. Maybe I'm incapable of love; if it were only simpler. Love slips through my fingers, I can't hold on to it."

Darkness was drawing in and it was cold, even in a warm, insulated ski outfit. "It's time I was off, Sasha," I said, "come and see me and we'll talk again. As for love I've remembered a poem by Andrey Dementyev. Listen:

When love departs forever
Bid farewell to her
You are free of your past
But not of your memory."

On the way back to my hotel I thought that it was good the man had got it off his chest. It would be easier for him now. *And let he who is without sin cast the first stone.* My hotel hovered into view. It was a small, three-storey building facing the main street. The owner was once a renowned mountaineer. He had participated in the first Italian expedition to conquer K2. Now he was an old man who often sat on the ground floor in the bar. The hotel was run by his sisters, two older women who wore black. They were assisted by two young ladies from west Ukraine, the hired help. They were both very chirpy and friendly. One of them was pretty alluring, I knew her shift would finish today and she had got dressed up and put on some makeup. I sat in the bar and ordered a coffee.

"Are you going somewhere?" I asked.

"Yes, in an hour my friend will take over and I'm free for the next night."

"Are you going to relax?"

"I've relaxed here," she said briskly, "the guy I'm seeing here, an Italian, won't let me rest. I've been working here for four years. I just go back and see my family in the summer."

"Do you have a big family?"

"Oh just a typically sized one, a husband and two children."

"And?" I opened and closed my mouth. This was the second multiple-partner merchant I had come across today.

The woman could tell I was taken aback. "Well, it's like this… my husband is there. I suppose he doesn't waste time missing me as well. We're saving up for a house. In a couple of years we'll build one for our children; and we'll need to give them an education."

"Who is looking after the children?"

"Grandma, who else? The whole family lives on my earnings. If he was a jealous guy he'd work himself and not send his wife out to work."

I studied her with grudging respect. It was the same variant only, so to speak, in the opposite direction. "Please don't be offended by my questions. This is your own business, your own burden." Unable to resist I asked, "This Italian, does he have a place in your soul?"

"My husband alone has a place in my soul," she replied drily, "otherwise I wouldn't have married him?"

So, this was really a different variation to that described by my friend. Life is indeed multi-faceted.

The bell on the front door rang and my group poured into the bar. They had been in the town and were quite merry but wanted to continue partying. We settled down around the hearth. The evening turned into amicable booze up. As hunters tell tales in the evening, so too our party told of the day's skiing. Someone was drawn into a few risky exploits but it all ended well.

A new day awaited us tomorrow. Before I retired for the night, I went out on to the street and looked into the sky. The full moon shone on high. Vast stars, like burning thorns, pierced a blindingly black sky; the heavens are very beautiful when viewed from the mountains. When you look at it during the night you realise that you are not only looking at the abyss, the abyss is looking at you. Men and women and their complex relationships become secondary to the power of nature.

The great German philosopher Friedrich Nietzsche spoke if this: a real man wants two things, work and play. That's why he needs a woman, as the most dangerous of playthings.

The Fly

"Granddad, a fly is buzzing around you," yelled my four year old grandson, "give me a newspaper, I'll swat it."

"Don't," my wife told him, "we don't kill flies. If we really have to we'll throw it out into the yard."

"Why not?" My grandson was not pacified by this advice.

"Because a fly once saved your granddad's life."

"This fly?" asked little Boris.

"Well, maybe not this fly but one like it?"

The event took place on thin ice, on the razor's edge. I will not speak of most of the details or even allude to them, but everything else I will tell you now is true. And it would be wrong of me not to speak of it because it is for you, little Boris, that I write this tale and this book. You will read it one day and we will be closer to each other.

It was summer in the year 2000 and an uncompromising struggle for survival was taking place in the world of banking. At least half of all economic activity was in the shadows. There were only a small number of good, legitimate clients and still fewer of those who were thriving. The banks fought among themselves, often with extreme savagery, for these few worthy individuals.

At this point I received some interesting information. As a result of intergovernmental agreements, one of our clients, a shipyard, might receive a large military order. We had discovered that there was a possible advance of ninety-million dollars and the total value of the commission could reach several hundred-million dollars. These were very alluring figures in those dark times. The payments could be transferred through a Ukrainian bank, i.e. ours, or through one of the Russian banks associated with this industry. There were a number of possible variations combining both these options.

We began to negotiate a meeting through our subsidiary. I understood that representatives of the Russian bank were also in talks with the shipyard management team. The managers, for their part, decided rationally to combine these negotiations. It would, in effect, create a preliminary tendering process.

We all gathered together at the factory to discuss it. The serious financial flows involved meant this was no frivolous affair. There were technical and technological problems to be resolved and each party obviously fought their corner. The friendly hosts did not make a final choice then. Indeed, it was not solely within their competence and the fight was shunted along to the next round. Throughout this time we lived exclusively on coffee, tea and biscuits. The talks ended at about five in the evening and everyone was invited to a feast and we went there with a huge appetite.

Twilight drew in and the table was set outside in the open air, for the Crimean August is swelteringly hot. I sat at the side of the table and the waiter approached, bearing a rectangular tray on which stood high-legged saucers brimming with salad. Approaching the table, he stooped and turned the tray at an angle towards me. He had an ice bucket with a bottle of champagne in the other arm. One of the saucers was directly opposite me, I got hold of it mechanically by one of its legs and placed it in front of me. The table was already set with a fork on the left and a knife on the right of me. I took the fork, scooped up some salad and bore it to my mouth.

Something was troubling me. My head of security was sitting at the next table; I looked around at him and he also appeared perturbed. *Something was wrong, but what.*

I turned my head again and looked at the salad. A large fly had seated itself on it and continued to do so. I no longer had an appetite and, swallowing what little there was in my mouth, I rose and went to the drinks table. I had a glass of vodka and some bread and butter and soon it was time to leave and eat something at home. I headed for my car, saying farewell to the other meeting participants on the way. While emerging from the restaurant's veranda I looked at the table; the bloody fly was still there, as if glued to the salad.

I arrived home half an hour later; I had something to eat and went to bed. I had not been asleep for long before I woke with violent stomach pains and was very seriously sick. I was not someone who was usually susceptible to food poisoning. Many years of wandering the world had tempered my body carefully for many years; I only ate unpretentiously and as necessary. As far as I was concerned food was just the process of ingestion. I was so ill an ambulance was called and it took me to hospital where I was given an injection and had my stomach pumped, but I got worse and worse. The doctor asked me if I had eaten any tinned food.

"What?" I replied

"It looks like botulinum poisoning. Well, forgive me, I don't know why you are still with us in this state," he said, falling into an expressive silence.

"No," I replied, "I had a perfectly ordinary dinner at home and yesterday at six o'clock I dipped into a salad at a restaurant."

A vague suspicion stirred inside me then. The waiter presenting that particular salad had manoeuvred the tray so my choice was restricted. That is what had troubled me the day before - and that weird fly. I asked them to allow my head of security to come to see me and explained the situation to him; I instructed him to go to the restaurant and have word with the waiter who had distributed the salads.

My recovery was slow. I was suffering from double vision, shortness of breath, extreme fatigue and tachycardia. Everything that could be inflamed was inflamed. I was injected with a serum of some kind and the poisoning eventually went into reverse. Three days later I was more or less back to some sort of acceptable condition. It was my fifty-fourth birthday and people visited me at home to congratulate me, but I could only greet my guests while lying on the sofa. Some complications still remained and I had to undergo a, not especially severe but an extremely painful, surgical operation as a result. For a couple of months I could only travel in a car while lying down; the seats were lowered to accommodate me. I had to write papers at work while standing - a special desk was made for me, which I still have. I made up some tale about how advantageous it was to work standing up. A few people even followed my example.

It took six months for me to recover my fitness. I was finally okay by the winter and went skiing with my daughter at Verbier, leaving all my troubles in the past.

Other events connected to my poisoning unfolded while I was recovering. My head of security did not find the waiter concerned. The restaurant said he had secured a job with them on the morning of the poisoning by presenting a letter of recommendation from the head of a renowned club. He had promised to bring his documentation the following day, but he never showed up and did not get paid for the one day's work he had completed.

"A letter?" my head of security asked.

"Yes, a letter, here it is."

We contacted the supposed author and signatory of the letter. It was the first time he had seen it.

None of the other participants at the buffet were harmed in any way, but the dog who resided at the restaurant and ate scraps from the tables had died in agony. We began to investigate the affair discreetly, but there were no leads. I tried to hire a Russian detective agency but they did not take up the case and would not explain why they shied away from it. We were at a dead end.

Time passed and everything slowly became history. The

Russian bank ceased to be in existence, falling at some point in the 'fatal struggle' of Russia's eternal crisis with capitalism. I wondered whether it was that bank that had poisoned me? There were serious doubts on that point. The case remained, as the investigators said, 'unsolved'.

When I had studied at the Odesa Electro-technical Institute of Communications in my youth, for a period I had been fascinated by cybernetics and information theory; I was captivated by some of the philosophical implications of what were then new sciences; by white noise, normal stationary noise. An old friend from this time came to visit me a year and a half ago. He had worked for many years in Moscow, carving out a good business career for himself. We talked about many things and he told me a tale: "I was sitting with a group in Sanduny, Moscow, celebrating something or other. There was another group at the next table, also having a good time. We exchanged a few words, they realised I was from Crimea and we got nostalgic about it. Your name bobbed up and the guys in the group suddenly became guarded. One of them asked if you were still in business and I told him you were in good health. He said you were lucky and asked me to pass on his regards. So, here I am giving you his regards," my guest said, "but I don't know from whom I'm giving them."

"I don't know either," I said, "but I would like to know."

I have never killed flies since that time. People are sometimes worse than flies. In any case that ship building contract imploded, there was no finance for it and no agreement helped. *You tried in vain to acquire it by bumping me off, sir!*

But it is entirely possible this is not the last word:

I said in mine heart, God shall judge the righteous and the wicked: for there is a time there for every purpose and for every work. (Ecclesiastes 3:17 King James Bible)

Lightning Source UK Ltd.
Milton Keynes UK
UKOW01f1148020817
306528UK00002B/366/P